not merely because of the unknown
that was stalking toward them

not merely because of the unknown
that was stalking toward them

JENNY BOULLY

Tarpaulin Sky Press Grafton, Vermont

2011

First Edition, 21 June 2011
ISBN-13: 9780982541678
Printed and bound in the USA
Library of Congress Control Number: 2011930265

Cover image: Noah Saterstrom, "Specter Projector", 22" x 30", mixed media on paper, 2010. From the collection of Ashleigh and Josiah Coleman. Please visit www.noahsaterstrom.com.

Tarpaulin Sky Press
P.O. Box 189
Grafton, Vermont 05146
www.tarpaulinsky.com

For more information on Tarpaulin Sky Press perfect-bound and hand-bound editions, as well as information regarding distribution, personal orders, and catalogue requests, please visit our website at www.tarpaulinsky.com.

For Penelope

If she lays out two spoons (two *real* spoons) and two forks (two *real* forks), will he come then to take part in a meal that is wholly *imaginary*? The food was never real, the food was never *really real* and so to send them to bed *without*, to send them to bed without a meal, hardly meant anything.

These things may fit inside a thimble: a pinch of salt, a few drops of water, the tip of a woman's ring finger. I will give you a thimble, says Wendy. I will give you a thimble so that you will know the weight of my heart. A thimble may protect against pricks, pin pricks, needle pricks, Tinkerpricks, but not hooks, never hooks. When he stabs his hook into you, you will see that his eyes are the blue of forget-me-nots—but that is Hook and not Peter—Peter who will forget you, whose eyes are the color of vague memories, the color not of sky, but rather of the semblance of sky, the color of brittle-mindedness, of corpse dressings, of forgetting.

The window was not left open; there was another boy sleeping in the bed. That is the story that Peter doesn't like to hear; that is the story he will tell you to get you to *forget* about mothers. Oh, Wendy,

---

The Home Under Ground

When she was two, Wendy knew she would die. The flower told her; her mother held her chest and gasped, asked for *forever. Two is the beginning of the end.* And when he stops coming for you, that is how you might know that things have *ended.* But on the island, the island made *real*, she is allowed to live after having died, because the boys would like for her mouth to remain *forever open. She is moving in her sleep. Her mouth opens. Oh, lovely!* Peter thinks that maybe she will sing in her sleep. *Wendy, sing the kind of house you would like to have.* And Wendy, with her eyes still closed, sings.

if ever you hear me speak about mothers, you must think I am truly speaking about lovers until I remember you. But we aren't really, *really* married, are we? The window hasn't been left open, and there is another boy sleeping in your bed. The absence of the beloved, the replacement that is easily replaced by Peter's mother is also easily replaced by Peter himself, who will *forget* you, who will forget to love you or even to *know* you. That bandage around his head that he came home with—if it wasn't you who wrapped it around there, who dressed his wound lovingly, then it must have been another wife, another girl, another mother, another papoose who isn't you.

He will come to you in the darkest part of night when you are sleeping and play upon his pipes until you stir; he will come to you to teach you how to fly so that you may visit that dark other space there between two stars. Despite his ability to *lose* so much, despite his boyish looks, his boyish charms, he can only dress himself with skeletons, with skeleton leaves; he smells of and is made of the loam of decaying roots and branches, the rotting sap and juices of Neverland trees. And what are these? What are these? asks Mrs. Darling, who knows that these leaves, these leaves littering the nursery floor, *these leaves* aren't the leaves of earthbound trees.

The Home Under Ground

Would the death boat be made of the feathers of the Never bird? Enclose her within the rib bones of swallows. And she can strew herself, and she can sew her own self a pocket, white and satin and somewhat ecstatic. That gleaming in his eyes isn't a personal excitement; if ever, if ever I forget you, then.

The pillows insisted on one bout more, like partners who know that they will never meet again. You can grow up; you can grow up and up and up and wear a tie and go to the office, and when you come home, to a house that is *above* ground, she will always have something in the cradle, for she must always have something in the cradle. Someone must be in the cradle. *I should love you in a beard.* And two spoons and two forks and two plates will be left out for a meal that you must eat, for a meal that will no longer be *imaginary*; however, the window has been left open again, and that question, on a rather sweet subject, has not yet been spoken. He did not take Wendy's thimble but rather Mrs. Darling's. It was Mrs. Darling's kiss that he left with.

If you were to ask her, before she had ever *really* gone there, what her Neverland was like, she would have mentioned her pet wolf. She would have mentioned this as if she had *been there. It's a wolf with her whelps. Wendy, I do believe that's your little whelp!* On the island made real, Wendy's pet wolf has no recognition of her, wanders about as if it has no need for a mother; it *is* a mother. And Wendy sometimes catches glimpses; Wendy sometimes hears it stirring about. (The *it* here may have more to do with connotations, with future imaginings, with a time in the not-too-distant future

---

The Home Under Ground

Old wolf: so *carnal*, all wrapped up in a kind of bestial hunger, a crossing over, all totemic and looming now. Why should he say that the little girl should *love* it? Don't you think 'tis strange? As if he wanted to suggest something about a true, albeit suppressed, nature. 'Tis not done, I'm sure, for *contrast*. So the death boat here would involve a belly of stones to weigh it down, to bring the wayward thing to drown.

when her unraveling hem—too short—will have risen, a rising tide water, way past her ankles and will not reach quite past her knees.)

The wayward thing, the wayward thing is not Wendy, but rather Tiger Lily, and *there is not a brave who would not have the wayward thing to wife.* But Wendy notices; she notices how Peter will go off to fight for her, will go off to reclaim her, to free her from pirate strings and pirate beams; he'll untie her with teeth, will carry her overboard, will safely stay underwater until there are no grown-ups in sight.

I'm a little bird, he says. *I'm a little bird that has broken out of an egg.* And dear Wendy, dear Wendy, who gathers all the bramble wires, the briars and twigs of the Neverland forest, who crouches down to make a little nest, who crouches down to make a little kindling for a fire, where is she to lay down this little bird who crows and crows and crows? When he talks in his sleep, he will say a name you have never known; there will be an *adventure*; there will be an adventure *without you.* When he talks in his sleep, you will know that one day, one day you will sleep and sleep and never wake, and he will go on. He will go on *without you.* Never mind that the daffodils are already a-wilting; never mind that you can no longer let out the hem.

The Home Under Ground

We won't notice that we've grown until we've grown: that's Wendy's predicament. Hook's: he won't notice that he's dead until he's dead, and the only reason now for his dying is Peter's having discovered the art of mimicry: Peter hadn't known he was tick-tocking, tick-tocking through his teeth; he hadn't noticed the tick-tocking until he realized that the thing coming to kill him wasn't lurking underneath.

The *elegant lady of uncertain age* will alight; she will alight aboard a train that carries so many years and brittle Neverland leaves with it. Oh, Wendy, who is she? Who is she? Leave out the details that occur, that occur only in the other realm: the hair gray here and there, the eyes a little less bright, the coarse hairs that just won't disappear, the soiled and soured undergarments, the curdled milk, the skin that won't pull itself tight. Oh, elegant woman of uncertain age, Peter will not *love you*—he will not love *you* in a beard, not in a corset, not in a standing room, not in a wedding dress, not in a bedroom, not when you are older than ten plus two.

So you see now he *appears* to be covered with fish scales; they're all tangled in his hair—in his head hair, in his cochlea hair, in the little tuft above his bum, in his pubis down. It was only an adventure, Wendy. It was *only*. But she knows the look of infidelity, knows the smell of a certain merlady. Who among them will live forever? Certainly not the girl who has been left at home; certainly not the girl who has been left darning socks alone. (The darning egg is really a stone.) *I'm a little bird*, he says. But he doesn't say that to just you alone. And now, the whole of the house a salt-water affair—his breath, his musk, his farts, all tinged with that certain crabby smell. I'm Wendy, she says. I'm Wendy. But it doesn't stop there:

The Home Under Ground

When she gets married, she gets married in a gown with a pink sash. She'll wear it for Peter, but who will know? She'll tell her husband, she'll tell him, I've never done this—I've never done this before. But when then does there appear to be so many prickly lights, so many minute butterflies alighting on the corpse? Has Peter come then? Has Peter come to take her, to take her half the way?

the bed all a-crusty, the floorboards all a-sandy, the bath basin all a-glittering with mermaid hair.

For now, we will just have to use what we have. The acorns can *stand in*; they can stand in for a meal. The one glass there can be passed; it can be passed round and round. Let's say there's medicine in it; let's say the tincture will bring you back if you drown. There are no other mothers; there are no other mothers around. We'll just pass Wendy round and round. She will make you a place that you didn't have before; she will make you a place that will be something to carry.

The dogwoods are opening ever-so-slowly.

(When you imagine Wendy, you must imagine her at her most lonely. She's twelve, then fourteen, then sixteen, then married. She'll leave the window open; she'll wear the same nightgown; she'll keep whispering stories, stories out the crack of the window, through key-holes, through fissures in the ground. Whenever she hears a twig snap or the fluttering wings of moths, she'll think that Peter's back, but he's never back, at least not for her. And in her diaries, she'll write that she had never really loved anyone. Else. In her diaries,

---

The Home Under Ground

Wendy knew, all along, that she would die. She had a song for it. *Sing us the kind of afterlife that you would like to have, oh, Wendy.* And Wendy sings. She sings the kind of afterlife that she would like to have, and in her afterlife there is her little house, and Peter and she are married— but not like before, but *more real*, in a marriage made more real, which meant that Peter, little bird, someday too would need someone to help him half way to a place hidden between two stars.

she'll write that she knew about *it* all along, knew about it but continued to love nonetheless.)

The living and the dead may always be one and the same to him. So when he kills you, he kills you so that he might be able to kill you again. And when he loves you, he loves you so that he might be able to love you again. These little acorns here: let's draw faces on them and pretend they are toy soldiers; let's make-believe they are the only food we'll ever have and *save them, save them*; let's say they are poison and you are the traitor and so it is you who must eat of them; let's bury them in the ground, tonight before bed, and overnight, they'll grow and grow and one day, they'll grow so fast and tall that they'll grow out of this world and we'll cut her down and make a fort of her. And Wendy, who grew so fast and so tall, who grew so that she could live only in another world, dreams of being a little acorn, a little heartbeat.

They are, however, allowed to change, only it must be a complete change. Tinker Bell who had room, but who only had room for just one feeling at a time, who could only be *this* or *that*, mad or happy, jealous or

---

The Home Under Ground

The Wendy girl will *live longer* than you; the Never bird will *live longer* than you; the wayward thing will be taken to wife (unlike you, who will never be *taken to wife*), and she too will *live longer* than you. Shoot her down, shoot her down, you say. And down comes the Wendy bird, and down comes the Peter bird to say *who has done this?* And you're shut up in your little house again, and all around you, the various fairy birds a-dying, a-falling away from the Neverland, hanging cocoon corpses in Never trees for the Never worm, for the Never bees.

content, could sometimes be brought back quite easily to life. Tink, the skeleton leaves are getting quite dirty, quite yellowed, quite wilty and your wings are all crinkled and saggy; your little light, your little light goes *out*.

Little Tink will hardly live; she'll hardly live for a season and a day. Peter, who loved her but only until a new mother came, was fond of shutting up. He was fond of shutting up Tink in her little house made of skeleton leaves. Poor Tink, who only wanted to sleep in Peter's bed again, who only wanted to love, however briefly, before she would have to die, for all fairies *have to die*, took her punishment and took it quietly and stayed shut up until Peter would *need her again*, until Peter would need her to save *his* life.

All are keeping a sharp look-out in front, but none suspects that the danger may be creeping up from behind. This shows how real the island was. From the look-out, if we part, if we part the branches of the willow, then we'll see that the pirate ship is docking; the pirate ship is docking by the clam-shell stone. The pirate ship is all a mass of bloody feathers, of broken bird bones. Smee, oh Smee, come down

---

The Home Under Ground

A nosegay can be used for *a little girl*; a little girl should have a nosegay. A bouquet may *overwhelm*. And what might Wendy's favorites be but the offerings of spring: budding branches of dogwood, of lilac, daffodils and cherry blossoms, forsythia and magnolia, hyacinths and tulips. When the seasons change and a little fairy dies and Wendy will never be quite as *little* again, she'll leave the window open; she'll leave the window open in hopes of a little, in hopes of a little dark space that she'll sew up and sew and sew and sew.

from your look-out and see how we too have prepared a little meal just for you; *just for you!* But the night is a-coming, and the night has nothing to do with pirate ships or pirate whips or pirate planks or pirate cannons or pirate stones or pirate crypts. (Oh, sink the cat. Sink the cat first. Sink the little cat first so we can see if this little trick works!) From the look-out, if we part the trees to see the stars, then we'll see that a ship is docking; a ship is docking by the clam-shell cloud. If we part the clouds to see, then we'll see a creature that breathes ever so slowly, so slowly you can't ascertain that it's even a creature at all, but you're in its belly; you're in its belly (the tick-tocking is *in a belly!*) and it won't ever, not now, not ever spit you out.

The little cake—it is *poisonous*. The little cake—it is *gorgeous*. Tootles, poor Tootles, who has never ever had a mother, wants to partake of the little cake. But it's all green now, all grown over with the green of moss and Neverland forest rot. The cake has grown; it's grown as hard as a stone. The pirates will still take it from shore to shore in hopes that the little boys will take it home for some birthday party or other, and they'll all die off, *one by one*.

The Home Under Ground

Mrs. Darling *remembered*. She remembered, but didn't quite want *to say*. She remembered, she said, *a certain* Peter Pan. *There were odd stories about him, as that when children died he went part of the way with them, so that they should not be frightened. But didn't you and Peter go all the way?* When he was with you, did he ever, ever make a promise *to stay?* The pregnancy may have only been *molar*, and the boy's second teeth may have never *come in*. So why should you fret then? Why should you fret when it is spring and the lilacs are all a-dripping *without you?*

Peter does some things to you, and after that you fit. For the house underground, he'll take your measurements; he'll see how tall, how wide is that tree and whether or not you'll survive without scratches, without getting stuck, going down. He'll find a tree; he'll find a tree *for you.* And then, thereafter, it will be *your tree,* all hollow on the inside. And a little bird will come and a little caterpillar will come and perhaps a little apple too will grow *for you.* Oh, Wendy, don't look now, but your dress is just a tad bit shorter *than it was when.* Do you think he'll notice? Do you think he'll notice when you droop a little, when you stoop a little, when you hunch a little on your way down? Peter does some things to you, and after that, you will want to fit; you will want to fit *forever.*

First, it will be the size of this here speck of sand, Wendy, and then, while you're asleep, that's when it will start to grow little feet. It will grow into the size of an acorn and then into something you can hold. We'll make-believe a bottle of warm milk for it; we'll make-believe the doctor's come to tidy things. But will it fly, like all of our

---

The Home Under Ground

By the fire, Wendy is a knitter, and Peter has taken to calling her *old lady. Ah, old lady, there is nothing more pleasant of an evening for you and me when the day's toil is over than to rest by the fire with the little ones near by.* She turns the heel, says, *I have now passed my best.* Old lady, old lady, even the fallen fruit looks more appealing than you; your chin, a wizened peach skin. Don't write down *what actually happened;* instead, write down *what you wanted to believe.* The words will crook and curl for you. So, when he says, *Yes, it is a dull beginning. I say, let us pretend that it is the end,* don't think he means *you* or *his love for you;* the end, after all, is something that, since the beginning, has been hovering.

other children, dear? It will fly, Wendy, and I'll always keep it. Here. And it will grow wild and unshaken; it will have a cloven foot and mane. My dear.

The rocking chair appears to be missing *a little something*. If you hang the birdcage there, we'll hear its singing. Keep the curtains sheer drawn over the four-poster—that's the kind of bed *I would like to have*. I will can the preserves; I will can the preserves so that come autumn, come autumn when I have hung up the dustpan, you will have this small bit of apricot to remember. Me by. I don't think I quite believe in *that* anymore, and besides, this here tooth has fallen; out; it's the last one I've needed for quite a while. I will cut the slices of apple *for you*; I will shake the grove of bramble bushes *for you*; the raspberries, too tart, too tart, I will lemon and sugar them *for you*, 'cause that is what mother has taught. My dear, did I write down all of my symptoms this morning? Has the paper been left right on our doorstep? I do believe, Wendy, I do believe that Smee has stolen it.

At night, the tulips close ever-so-slowly.

The Home Under Ground

And what does the message in the bottle say? It says that somewhere, somehow, new lives, new lives have sprung. And is it? Is it you, Wendy? Who has *sprung*? Why, yes. Why, yes, Peter, just now; just into this here new life now. But Hook's Jolly Roger says that someday, I will wither away, I will wither away down there, planted in a deep well in the sea. So why not then, Wendy? Why not *enjoy* this here vase of flowers? Why not serve with our serving spoon and the other silver wedding things?

Just throw it out, Wendy, that message in a bottle. But the little seed, I think, has stuck; the little ivy leaves, the little root shoots are *implanting*. They'll overtake the whole hull of the ship. Very carefully, Peter, you placed your little flag. On top. Now, something has come and corked it all. Up. Do you think? Do you think that the savage princess will help, will help with the uprooting of this little seed? Didn't your last will-of-the-wisp die just like this, just because of this? Little Michael will outgrow, will outgrow the bassinette. The little seed, Peter, the little seed is already wanting to climb toward the Never sea.

Tiger Lily: she has been a-tanning. Tiger Lily, Peter will come to *catch* you; he will come to hunt you; he will show your father that he knows whatever there is to know about straining a willow sap cord through the holes of your wigwam. He will, as promised, *keep her*. Warm. Tiger Lily: she has been a-rubbing so much of the lard of last month's boar kill on her bosom. See, there, they're all a-shiny, all a-glistening underneath the Neverland sun. Tiger Lily: her thong is all encrusted with the little shells from the sea shore: a little sand dollar here, a flake of fish scale, a scallop shell, a baby

---

The Home Under Ground

It was not, she knew, that night had come, but something as dark as night had come. No, worse than that. It had not come, but it sent that shiver through the sea to say that it was coming. The smile, the smile should give something away. If you had two of these, would you? Give one away? Down there, the beautiful sharks have lace-clogged gills. If you drown the baby, one will come up and up. The bassinette is all a-ready, all a-loaded with the dead weight of Neverland rocks. Let's try the papoose. Let's try the papoose first if already you don't know. How.

oyster, a clam broken into a myriad of sandy flecks, a little barnacle to show where. Tiger Lily: she doesn't shave her pubes, and they're all sticking out and out. But not too much, not very many: it's just a light crow-down feathering. And will you, Peter, will you say to her, when her father isn't looking: let's go to the lagoon, and let's play pretend that I save you right before. We drown.

And he has been gone five days now. The lost boys huddle all together by the hearth in Wendy, in Wendy's home. New stumps done grown. How, without Peter, will they pluck them out? And he has been gone five days; the pirates make frightful noises overhead. They stomp and stomp and stomp, use their very whiskers to feel out the hidden place. Who dares to light a fire or start the stove? Smee will sneeze, will sniff them all. Out.

Hook: his beard all a-sooty, all thick and black and damp and curly, all sort of pubic-y. The girl Wendy, the girl Wendy, looks about for a darning stone. The curling knife, the curling knife should want to tickle your funny bone. Let me show you, girl Wendy, what this compass, what this isinglass is for. Should you not like this bunker?

The Home Under Ground

Wendy, she gives the quiz in past tense. *What was the colour of Mother's eyes, and so on. Wendy, you see, had been forgetting too.* For lovers, the past tense may signify a corrosion of both language and time. For the lost boys, it signifies only a new item washed up on the seashore and that they had forgotten, they think, to eat. What was peach cobbler like, when we had it? What was the sand-grit flavored when we baked it into a cake? Was the cake then, that one, real or pretend? It's hard to remember when chocolate here always tastes like *chocolate*, when you think *of it*. Who last blew the candle *out*? Who last turned ten?

~ 13 ~

Should you not like this cannon fire? I should lock you, leave you alone among our preserves of apples and cider. Smee, his fist so far down the salted fish barrel; his fist so full; he thinks no one should be *looking*.

Say, Wendy! You've white cotton panties! Rufflely and lacey. Say, are they *bloomers*, maybe? But they are her *only* pair, and they could, lately, use a *real* rather than a pretend washing. They have attracted all manner of clawing: scorpions roost there; crabbies dig there; sea turtles lay there; little hands reach up and grab there. So, sometimes, when you want to get a whiff of her, she will glare. What lately has gotten into you, old lady?

Not rum, but rather, the *miasma of night*; that's all the pirates drink and need to stay. Alive. Over the bulwarks, they drink. And Hook, so *dejected*, so horribly alone. He's all alone, he thinks, because no one, not even the Flint, can take on *a good form*. How shall he address the

---

The Home Under Ground

Wendy, in her song about the kind of house that she *would like to have*, sings that she would like to have *roses peeping in, you know, / And babies peeping out*. There were no Neverland roses. The boys all come together and agree to the latticing of the make-believe. They'll make-believe roses all around the perimeter of Wendy's home, which is a home *above ground*. But they did not want any more babies to be peeping out; they didn't want any more babies. So quickly, quite quickly they sing back to the girl Wendy, *We cannot make ourselves, you know, / 'Cos we've been made before*, and that, they think, will prevent Peter from the ordering of anymore babies. They could not make themselves, because they had been made before. You know; you should know. They've been *made before*.

envelope? How to word the invite? Dearest Wendy—I am inviting you to sup with…Dear Wendy, your presence is …Should he have little Tootles deliver? *Poor kind Tootles, there is danger in the air for you to-night. The big thing* will happen*; it will happen just as you* step aside. Dear Wendy, please come; Hook would like. To see. You. He takes on the third person, the third form. Her little ankles, all dirty with Neverland dust.

Dearest, I will arrange the teapots so that they are just so, just so. If the water in there is all a-murky, it's because it was collected back then; can't quite remember just when; the pond-skater all at home in it just now. As for the little tadpole—he's gone away; he's gone away into a belly. No tea, but rather; that's all we children need to stay. Alive. I do believe that there's a little mole scratching up there. A badger, a claw-y glow worm. There are tree branches and tree roots somewhere down there all a-meshed with the hair of our newborn. Get me the scissors, but the cord is up there, way up high, there between the space of those two stars. Perhaps, perhaps, Peter,

---

The Home Under Ground

Come autumn, should we plant a grove of peaches and pears and red delicious? Perhaps, perhaps the food could be less *non-existent?* I think that Slightly's teeth are falling out quickly simply due to mal-nutrition, mal-eating. But Peter simply doesn't want to plant *anything*. Permanent, he says. Then maybe, then maybe, says Wendy, maybe we could plant some bulb flowers, some perennials so that come spring, come spring, you will know that you will have to *come for me*. And should the bulb and the bulb's offspring live quite way well into the miasma of night and some spring when I *come for* to find that you are there no more, what then? What then, girl Wendy? The spring blooms: they too will outlive. You.

you could. Take. Me. Dearest, I will brew the medicine so that it is just so, just so. If you think there's a sort of metallic tinge, if you think there's a certain bitterness, it's because the root was collected way back; when; can't quite remember just; the little bean sprout all at home in it just now. Oh, look! Look! Dig up the root: it's all a-hairy! Dig up the root if already you don't know how.

The miasma, the miasma of night is between your legs, Wendy. I do say! Do you think Hook can have a *look? No little children love me!* says he. Why, Hook. I do. I do *love you.* And that is why the answer is in the *affirmative.* You see, Wendy, I must put you in chains so that you don't fly. Away. Because you might, that is, fly away. (The line seems unconscious of her presence.) But *only,* only if you love me *only.* The plank, all slick with salt water—what if, what if I should *slip?* Johnny Corkscrew: all a-twisted and a-curved, feeling out now that certain *funny spot.* It will make you *laugh* but just a little. A second time and then a third and then the *unhappy Hook was as impotent as he was damp, and he fell forward like a cut flower,* his eyes all a-glistening with Neverland mist, Neverland byes. And now, oh dear!, how he snores, how black flags and stormclouds fly.

The Home Under Ground

Two is the beginning of the end. As in, *you* and *me,* Peter; we make *two* and the story, and the story takes on an *and then.* The Never lilacs—they too do not live. Forever. The vase water all stagnant, all murkish brown now. I say, Peter, we should have *changed* it, but for your pet frog that swam there; ol'boy: even he's all dead now. *Two is the beginning of the end.* And mother's kisses, which I miss, falling one after the other, one hidden in the other, so that there was always another. *However many you discover there is always one more.* Tinker Bell: she's all locked up now, but when she comes out, she too will give you such a fright.

Dear Peter,

you may *think* that when I sewed you back your shadow, that I truly did sew back your shadow, but now, I am confessing that I did not, have instead held onto it for the whole while of these years. I will slip this into my Margaret's nightie; I know, you have been a-footing about her floorboards, her satined bed. You will find it; you will, I know, look into her pockets. Dear Peter, have you even learned yet how. To read? Your little boy shadow: he *laughs like you!* He flits about, like you; he's frantic, like you; he wants to sit in my lap, like you, but sometimes, he runs away, too. Dear Peter, he has *your* eyes. I have shut him up in a drawer to save *for you.*

— I'm *Wendy.*

On a walk through the Never woods, you may encounter a certain kind of *evidence.* Tiger Lily: her footprints make little angel-hand imprints, leave a dusting like pearly oyster sand. On a walk through the Never woods, you may indeed encounter a certain kind of evidence: Tiger Lily feet that meet with Peter Pan feet *just there*, right there betwixt that pile of Never leaves. And a strand of wet pearls;

The Home Under Ground

Wendy may *like* Hook; she may have mistakenly left her pink sash out there for him to find come high tide. Hook, your belly is all a-hairy; it's a little distended there from all your whale eating. He suggests that maybe perhaps he go on a diet different from his other men; he says he should like to eat a little muscle, a little muscle with nary a beard. Wendy, grown oh-so-rebellious now from having flown out the window, says, I will dig the hole, Hook; I will start making the rounds.

and a slick leather band; and a totem animal toy signaling some-thing towards the Never clouds. Peter at home: ruffled feathers, a broken arrow, a smudge of red clay all down his back.

Peter, there must be some sort of *allergen*. Do you think, Peter, do you think Tink has been spreading some sort of bacterium around here? I can hardly get *out*. Of bed. She has a certain aversion to *wild-wood pollen*, but the girl Wendy doesn't quite know it. Yet. The bed sheets, the blankets, the pillowcases, they're fairly misted with the spores of the Neverland forest. In a few days, there will appear there a blanket of fungus, a thicket of huckleberry bushes. Peter, you've been bringing certain critters to bed, have you? Have you, my dear? The little allergen, it's so *tiny*; it doesn't quite yet have. Hands.

Let us pretend now to grow an herb garden and a fruit orchard and a vegetable patch. We'll have all manner of gourds and climbing things and things that take root, like radishes and carrots and beets. What do you say, dear Wendy? I do. Say, Peter, that *that* is a *splendid*

The Home Under Ground

What I wanted to give you was this here little tiny piece. Of me. If it heals; if it heals *properly*, it won't leave. Such a scar. Where it's red, it's only red for just a little. While. Return soon. To normal it will. The message, the message in a bottle, hasn't been claimed by anybody, and soon, soon those pirates, a-marauding they will go; they'll rip that parchment to pieces, and who then will know? Some night, in dream, when I will have climbed the look-out, it won't be you who I see, but rather another more distant star, another darker molting of sky. And so you will lie. And I will not be there too—not in a hovel, not in a bottle, not in a happy-ending novel, not in a kitchen serving eggs for two, and certainly not in a parallel grave from you.

idea! Splendid! Splendid! Splendid! I will have to *stay*. I will have to stay to see just how our crops are getting on. Getting on. And then maybe, every year, come spring, in addition to dusting your shelves, scouring your pans, and sorting out your little boy things, I can hoe and till and dig and bury all manner of seeds. But what about? What about *flowers*? Should we make a path where they will be? Lilacs and tulips—I daresay that that should just about *do it*. And each spring, when they bloom, when they bloom, Peter: you better not. Forget. Me.

Oh, dear! Something, something is making me *sneeze*. No, I do not think, I do not think that it is something from the flowerbeds or Never weeds. Do you think there is a creature in the Neverland forest that we have never chanced to meet?

So should I? Wait? Should I keep waiting here for the first star to *appear*? The elegant lady of uncertain age leans on her windowsill in wait for the first star to appear so that she may wish she may, so that she might wish she might. Have. And the wish she wishes: the same as. *As soon as the door of 27 closed on Mr. and Mrs. Darling, there was a commotion in the firmament, and the smallest of all the stars in the Milky Way screamed out: "Now, Peter!"* The smallest and the

---

The Home Under Ground

The treasure is buried *here*, she says. She says it as if she has said it before. But that's *yesterday's* treasure, says he. He says it as if she has said it before. I want *today's* treasure; nothing personal, Wendy. Today's treasure will not need to be rubbed down to *make it shine*; it will come out all a-gleaming, so fresh I'll be able to see my own pearly teeth. In it. So then? So then, Wendy.

youngest of the stars that first cried out, how grown now is that star? Does it still urge the boy on or has it too grown glassy-eyed and old and weak? Wendy devises a plan: each night, she'll leave the window open and then alight from the 27's front door only to reënter through the side door. She'll wait then on the nursery room floor.

Meals: Mother Wendy lays down the rules. Rule No. 1: there will be no hitting back. But poor Tootles: he's too big and fat and his elbows, even when eating make-believe, push against the other boys and smack. Rule No. 2: should you have something to speak out against, politely raise your right arm and declare that you *complain of so-and-so. Is your mug empty, Slightly darling? Not quite empty, mummy.* I complain of Tootles, who has with his big hand, knocked over my milk mug; I will require more milk, mummy. And father, who is not sitting at the head of the table nor the foot of the table nor anywhere else; and father, who is not sitting with a tray somewhere else alone; and father, who has not come home for several days now; the girl Wendy is left to *mother* alone. And where has father *gone to*, gone to, mummy? Can you, your brood, feed? Tootles says that he would like to be father and if he can't be father,

---

The Home Under Ground

See, Nana knows to play dead, to *play dead*. Can we all beat the game if we, if we all play dead? Maybe, we'll play instead at being *grown up*, which is, you know, quite close, quite close. We'll play that we're sticking this here glass thing in your mouth, Wendy. No matter; don't fret that it's been in your mother's and her mother's and great-grandmother's too, and soon, quite soon, so much sooner than you think, it too will be in the mouth of your daughter's and then your granddaughter's too. Oh, boy! *I'm a little bird!* I crow and crow; just for you, Wendy; just for you.

well, then, he should like to pretend at being baby. *I don't suppose, Michael, you would let me be baby?* Michael, make room, make room. Something anon is coming with smaller feet than you.

And what shall I mark today as? Is it still a summer month? Or do months too reign strange in the Never wood? I think I will in this vase here put in a little pea for each day, a little *plea* for each day here. And what size *were* mother's thighs? Peter, this, even you *should know.* Try, try to *remember.* Should I begin then to keep a journal? Let's see. Perhaps first I should write all the stories, all the stories, Peter, that attracted you to me. If I have forgotten the stories, what then, what then? Why, then, you would surely leave. Me. And then maybe a few recipes for making cider and jelly so that the boys might have something other than make-believe. What's that you say, Peter? You don't know *A from Z?* Very well, very well, then, *for me.*

The Home Under Ground

Peter at it *again*: his nightly communication with the stars. You see, Wendy, they watch *me*. And if there should happen to be a silent and dreadful place, I'll tell them to fill it up, to fill it up with something. For the meanwhile, there is you, and your nightgown swishes! Oh, how it swishes like a foam! A dead white cocoon foam. You are milky and salty and sudsy, and I daresay, Wendy, that something is rising from the Neverland loam; perhaps it will be a new glowing mushroom that we can feed. To Smee. That adventure is a good one! The one in which we watch Smee turn things into other things. He'll say a great big stone is a great big tortoise: you see, Smee too can sometimes do make-believe. I daresay, Wendy, that something is rising from the Neverland loam, and I have made clothes of it; I have eaten of it; I have made communion with it: the stars, they watch *me*.

Poor, Tink! She has been stealing Wendy's peas; they're all spilling forward, out from her lantern house; she's been trying to hide more in the abandoned nest of a Never tree, where the birds eat them, where the caterpillars eat them, where Smee has found them and eats them. Poor, Tink! She thinks that this will cause the girl Wendy to leave, to leave, but Wendy, seeing her vase so sparse, so empty, thinks, oh, well, it seems that I have been here hardly, hardly for a few days at all and so longer on stays the girl Wendy. And one night, when Peter has gone out, the Tinker Bell goes to the girl Wendy in her sleep, says, Follow me, Wendy. Peter's in trouble. And so follows the girl Wendy.

Who among us has got the syphilis? The medicine. I think we do have a medicine for it; no, wait; this one here is for the tetanus and was administered last to Slightly who complained of Curly, Curly

---

The Home Under Ground

Miss Mermaid has a fair amount of skin *showing*. Tiger Lily hardly knows just how to wear underwear. It is *vulgar*—she thinks is something that mother might say. And poor Tink, Peter has locked her up *again*! Peter has ordered that she be sent away into her little skeleton cage for five nights and six days, *again*! And her little life—so short!—being spent away all locked up in her Never cage. Dearest Tink, should you and I together *unionize* against the Peter? Equal pay for equal work, we'll say. We'll say. Because we don't like those times when he plays at *favorites*, at least not with any one else. We would all like some *benefits*, we'll say. And what about *old age*? Have you, Peter, a pension plan for us? Shall there be a point system for how many times you'll come to visit? Well, except for poor Tink who'll be dead sometime before the end of this year.

having stabbed him with his dinner fork. I do complain of itchy crotch, says Tootles. I do complain. And all around, the lost boys are a-raising their hands; we *do* complain. I complain of pus and of the scurvy. Yes, yes, we do. We do complain. Let us then pretend that a new medicine has been sent. Let us say that, once taken, it will cure in precisely an hour and a day. You see, boys, says Wendy, what you need are *oranges*. Yes, Wendy, we have lately been getting them from the Tiger Lily. See here, a whole barrelful full. But when it's the girl Wendy who lies ill, will you, Slightly, again then play at being doctor? Tootles, again, complains of Peter; Tootles would like to play at being doctor.

Sometimes, though not often, he had dreams, and they were more painful than the dreams of other boys. So let us see then, Peter, how will you fare when there is no one here to *wake you*? You will dizzy yourself

---

The Home Under Ground

The weather, I think, must be changing. Was it, when we left, the cusp of summer and autumn? The smell of snow now. Nana, Nana, Nana, have you still the best ears? It's not your fault that a boy could be so quick, *so quick*! The Peter has such a magical flick of the wrist. Oh, Nana, are you, just now, prancing in the snow? My coat, I can see it, hanging in the wardrobe. Oh, was it black? Or maybe red. Or maybe. Do you think it will, this year, fit me? Nana, don't you daresay, at my homecoming, that I have *grown*. There will be no talk about my *growing*. I will still sleep in the nursery bed; Mother must let me! And, oh dear, don't tell anybody about how I have stolen every thimble in town. When a cusp is full, it is full to brimming. (Nana, Nana, Nana, I'll secure my feminine diaper to you; I'll say that you are the one who is menstruating!) The smell of snow now; acorns all about my feet.

with thinking of how you came *to be*. Here. And what if really no one should *love* you? Perhaps if we imagine a certain scenario: let us say that Peter did not cheat, and he's been carousing because he knows yet pretends not to know that Wendy will one day become *outgrown*. Let us say that the Wendy girl is the one he loves and that he loves her *alone*. And so, when he comes home, to a home that is under ground and laughs when there is want to weep and sleeps above the coverlet when there is want of the girl Wendy, then we know that it is because he dreams the dreams that are not the dreams of other boys. His dreams are *his* and *his alone*. Wendy, I say that one day, you will stop coming to me when it's dark and it's nighter than night and the pirates have been a-wanting to kill me and something dead and dreadful too—wanting. To kill me. The dawn now, all the color of yams of carrots of radishes of rhubarb of beets. All down by the mermaid lake, all along the trail of tee-pees, all along the shore where the pirates make a fire and bake us a pretty cake, I didn't leave. I didn't leave even one imprint of my little feet. This, Wendy, you must believe.

The Home Under Ground

Wendy sews Peter a blanket made of skeleton leaves; it matches his clothes; it will keep. Warm. His little feet. It's getting *colder*, I think. I can smell it, I think, the Never snow, the bare Never trees. And will you leave me here with my stove all make-believe, my make-believe chimney? It's so cold, so cold, and my house all slatty and latticey. The morning glories, the snap peas, the various gourds done finished creeping, and still, and still the wind's let in when it blows. Something, somewhere is getting *older*, I think. I can smell it, I think, the rusty hair, the brittle feet, an eggshell that's been left, that's been left in an abandoned nest alone.

And when the eclipse comes upon the island here, will you, like the other animals and creeping things, go into hiding? According to the star charts I have seen, it will occur on precisely the 16th of some month or other. But how do you know? How do you know, Wendy? It is only according to the star charts that I have *seen*. It must have been glimpsed when I was still on the other side of things. She does not mention the compass, the cutlass, the astrolabe, or the other instruments of navigating the sea.

I will sew a Never quilt *for you*; I will sweep the floor *for you*; I will dust the cupboards, empty the waste basket, shake the rugs and bang the dust out of the mattress *for you*. I will clear the cobwebs, water your flowerbeds, sweep the hearth, polish the silver *for you*. I will ready the bath, do the wash, hang it all out on the Never trees *for you*. And should I frame a picture? A picture of me? Keep still.

The Home Under Ground

He will not *thimble* you, girl Wendy. He has something else *to give*. What is that you say? That something has come *undone*? Undone? Perhaps it is merely bootstraps; perhaps it is a food wrap; (perhaps he's brought something sweet and delicate just for you!; a Linzer tart?; perhaps; perhaps!; perhaps he's got a little kitty grave just *for you*!); perhaps it was only the unbuckling of sky. And how long have you been counting seconds to see, to see just how long this would. Last? Surely the cake done baked by now. By now, the chicken has surely been de-feathered, all the shrimp neatly de-veined. Wendy, you see, I will give you *real* food to eat, but first, do you have something sweet for Jas Hook to drink? He will lay. He will lay certain things all out, all out: a pitcher with a spout, a bit of bratwurst, a gravy boat, a herring bone. By now, the sky done rent into a hundred pieces; by now, the lost boys, Mrs. Darling, the little bird: all must be wondering why she isn't home.

Keep still here. I've something in a thimble *for you*. Mementos: a lock of Peter hair, some Neverland sand, and should I try, should I try to swipe some fairy dust from the palm of your hand? So later some night when I am quite grown and alone I can try to fly. Back?

Oh, what, oh what *can* we do if we haven't got a thing to do? Why, you can help me wash your bearsuits, says Wendy. But the lost boys protest: they haven't taken off their bearsuits since. Don't you think, says Wendy, don't you think there is something strange and cruel about Peter making you. Wear them? Especially in this here August heat? But the lost boys, what can they say? They haven't known; they haven't ever known. They only do what Peter says. And Tootles, poor Tootles, who always misses an adventure, Tootles, we all know when his belly has a little grown; his bearsuit fairly stretches tightly over his tummy. I complain of Peter, he says, who makes us wear these bearsuits, but none of the other boys join in.

The Home Under Ground

Do you sense, dear, a certain *something*? Like a hand that keeps? That keeps on *interfering*? I wonder what would happen if not. Would we still all be here, free to do and choose? Then, I choose you, Peter, you of the pearl teeth, you of the skeleton leaves, you of the mourning doves. See, Tootles has to go. He has to go peepee, and that isn't, I daresay, *in the story*. He'll not climb out of the house under ground, but rather he'll just pee in that ole corner there and some of the pee will come and splash up on his feet and then he'll just return to bed and go to sleep as *if*, as if he didn't just pee on his floor, as if he didn't have any pee on his feet. Or take the baby—Michael lately has taken to sticking his finger up his pooper hole and then up his nose: that certainly isn't going to make it *in*. I daresay: there *is* a certain hand *intervening*.

(And how many children has she, has she? Let's see, there's Tootles and Nibs and Slightly and Curly and then the Twins. And Peter is the daddy and come lately are Michael and John, with Michael being the baby. And the tree underneath which they sleep curls and curves like an English sycamore, but not really. Not really.)

How cruel, how cruel he has been to Nana. He has placed the whole of his medicine in her drinking pan, and she will have to drink lest she get thirsty and what then? Mr. Darling: all in a flummox simply because, well, of *anything* really. (My dear, says Mrs. Darling, I just don't think I would like to, here, incorporate *anything* that the critics have got to say.) Mr. Darling: all in a flummox simply because.

The Home Under Ground

Don't let the Peter bird fool you (*fool you!*): he indeed knows how to read. A *certain code*. There are *certain books* for the learning in *his library*. But you haven't the key; you haven't the right words. Don't let the Peter bird fool you: he already knows that you will end in a realm of forgetfulness. You, the girl Wendy, no more useful than the rings on a Never tree, the rings on the oldest of the oldest Never tree even; you, the Wendy girl, no more useful than the layers of Never sediment, the husks of Never lobsters, the new year conch shell grown a little larger now. The little hermit crabs say that they too have buried themselves below ground; they too have peeled off an old skin; they too will need a new home now that they too done grown, done grown. The old fur doesn't fit; doesn't fit anymore, Wendy girl. And all your books and all your stories, why mother is taking them; she's taking them to some orphanage for girls. And Peter loved you for them and for them only. Somewhere in the Never trees: your old skin, your old skin in the wind done blown.

Some men would have resented her being able to do it so easily, but it was all a bit second nature to Mrs. Darling, all this knot tying: thirteen types of knot tie could she: the reef, the figure eight, the bowline, the sheet bend, the clove hitch, the common whipping, the butterfly, the eye splice, the oysterman's stopper, the single hitch, the thief, the thumb, the true lovers. She had, after all, learned how to do so from a certain sea cook, a Jas Hook, who she simply, as time wore on, called James. James, James, Darling James. James, James who didn't seem to mind it too much when her nightgown outgrown. *This* man now: all a sorry excuse for one. His tie won't tie he says and if his tie won't tie well then he simply won't be able to go to dinner tonight

---

The Home Under Ground

The girl's hair now so wild, all a mess of corn silk from a baby corn flush plucked. They've stolen a mess of them yesterday from the field of braves. Ole Tootles having a time. And the cow that lately wandered here being whetted for milk, and the twins turn-taking with the butter churn. Ole Tootles having a time with so much crème. He thinks he remembers something now about mothers. I do believe, Wendy, says he, pulling down on a teat, I do believe that I recall something about mothers; his bearsuit all foamy. But Wendy doesn't dare tell him; leaves him to quite believe what he pleases. The milk pail all salty and frothy by now. I do say, with all this teating and butter pounding that we've all taken on a rosy complexion; why our cheeks are quite the picture of strawberries and crème, which reminds me. Better take care of that skin, an old lady once told me. Someday, the girl Wendy's hair taking on a dried brittle cornhusk quality; the sun a big, burning something sunk down in the corn field; a Never piglet lost its mother, and a Never locust and a Never katydid circling something fierce; a dark pirate song miasma creeping in. It's about time. It's about time, says the girl Wendy, that we go in.

and if he isn't able to go to dinner tonight well then he won't be able to go to the office and if he isn't able to go to the office well then he'll lose his job and if he loses his job well then we'll all be out on the streets and we will all starve. All of this, to him, is a great *adventure*. And that is why, to him, Nana simply can't be nurse, can't any longer at night be brought in. With the children, he will try to play about in the nursery; he'll hoist young Michael on his back and play at sailing through the air, but that has, to the children, who lately have learned to fly, become oh-so-boring. But we are romping! We are *romping*! says Mr. Darling. Oh dear, oh dear, thinks Mrs. Darling, perhaps *ever after* should not happen, should never have happened *here*. She will show him the shadow; she will keep the shadow to her bodice pinned. He looks rather like a scoundrel, Mr. Darling says. He has the look of a scoundrel about him. Uh huh, says Mrs. Darling, that's him! That's him!

Something surely turning out strange with the formatting. Can't quite seem to get the space just right. The spacing quite off and

---

The Home Under Ground

Skylights: he didn't *last* long. How long was he there? I think it must have been the space of three sentences. But that is the storyteller's way—to kill simply to show you how it is done. The body kicked aside, the cigars unmoved, and the pirates simply keep on, keep on. That is what the storyteller has done, Wendy. (You didn't last *long*: the space of a *story*. If ever you think that the Hook is doing something or that Peter is doing something, you must remember that it is the storyteller who is doing something.) Morgan Skylights: we don't quite know anything else. And the pirates and the storyteller move on, move on. Skylights: he gave one screech.

these two stars here too far apart, not quite where they should be. It's happening all over I do believe. But do not despair—do not ever despair. If this here storyteller isn't quite right, why then, another, I do believe will shortly come. It's been known to happen. It's been known to happen, my dear. That's great, Wendy, because I do believe that I don't quite like *this* storyteller. I do think, Wendy, that I would like to hear one of your stories. Make it a story with *us* in it, something that I can't quite remember. Make it an *adventure*, Wendy.

Do you know the difference between real and make-believe? The Peter bird does not. He can have make-believe sex and think he's having real sex, and that is what is so great about the Peter bird. You haven't to worry about all that chaffing. And that, I think, is why the

---

The Home Under Ground

The crocodile too, passes, passes, moves on. You could, you know, smother. The tiny sound with leaves. That's how quiet the sound of it was on the island. That's how come the little peas kept *disappearing*, and why, and why each new leaf showing on the Never trees was carrying a semblance of *just having been there all along*. (Why? Why don't you talk, Peter, about your dead brother? I think that's the story *we would like to hear*! And see how you've even adopted his stance, his gait, his habit of playing pipes, that certain twitch in your ears.) Wendy will find her way by *following*. The beast will lead her to Jas. Hook, always. He will call her *my beauty*. But it is much more interesting to think of the gagging: *he was so frightfully* distingué, *that she was too fascinated to cry out. She was only a little girl.* Hook fingering a stack of cards; Wendy's finger on the dirty glass, inscribing: *dirty pig, dirty pig.* She, like her boys, staring only at the plank. Give them, Wendy; give them a mother's last. Wishes.

Tiger Lily has never gotten. Their make-believe is pretty amazing, but don't tell Peter that I told you that. What's that you say? He doesn't do it to you *make-believe*? Well, then, that would explain it then; that would explain *many* things. Attachment, for instance.

Did you know that the little shells are breaking? It's about that time when the shells start breaking. New birds done hatched, done grown, done flown. They've hardly anything in their newborn food sacs; they're still waiting to grow a belly. Here too, a gale that will come and kill them. All. Tomorrow, we'll find them all crushed on the Never ground, and Nibs can calculate how many, how many. Perhaps we'll take to playing doctor and stick a glass thing in. Glass thing will say they're dying. Or about to. Too dark, today even, for the tulips to open.

They don't quite believe in spring just yet, just yet. And a new moon tonight and a dark wave there and a Jolly Roger shadow cast here and there and everywhere. And ole Smee there up in the look

---

The Home Under Ground

You see, Wendy, I can take you part of the way, but I won't go *all the way*. With you. I will do this so that you will be *less afraid*. There will come a time, Wendy; there will come a time when even father will talk less and less to you, but you needn't sulk and hide in your room all day. That will just be the way it is; that is just his way. You needn't wait for me anymore all day. Oh, yes, you see, it is quite *dense*, but haven't you? Haven't you a good writing day, Wendy? I am only *quite sorry*, so sorry that this drawer won't open anymore. I daresay that something of me is tucked up inside of it. And I know. I know it isn't a matter of having a key or prying.

out—his mind not quite right; he'll do it; he'll do it so that it won't matter to him a bit. Do we even have a washing board and a basin to wash our clothes in? I suppose, I suppose we'll all just have to go around all stinky until we die. Little cocoons are breaking. Red turnips in my hands have come up too early and are breaking. The Never badger, the Never mole, I daresay they're trying to dig their way in! Should we, with these sticks, poke them? You ought not to judge anyone; who's to say they're not dreaming a little dream, too? A mushroom head here, a celery stalk there, three new baby bird graves, a fiddlehead here; places in the earth are breaking.

By the fireplace, Wendy is telling stories. Wendy is a storyteller. Do you think, Peter, that one day, you will get bored with my stories

---

The Home Under Ground

We might, in fact, *die here*, says he. That is the one thing that isn't quite on this island make-believe. Sometimes, you did find a body that you didn't dare go near. Even the Never flies, then, partaking of a real feast. And have you held someone else? Like this? Like how you're holding me? When the tidewater comes, the girl Wendy will sink. Or the sharks will come; the sharks too are not make-believe. Who among us will live forever? Why then should the kite come? For me? Because you make a great toast, Wendy, and all the world would like to have some of your toast and a bit of jelly. I believe a mother is someone who always contains two things. In your case: a little cat and some water. And already, is it Tuesday? That means it is a day for going into the weather to your office, my dear. And your salary will feed and feed and feed; that is where food and babies come from, come from. Don't you think, Wendy, that it is a strange and demonic thing: in the theatre, grown women play at being *me*? That's disgusting, says Wendy.

and then send me on home? Send me packing? Tinker Bell's little light dimming now. To think: I've been here the whole of a fairy's life. And you will remember her, only *vaguely, vaguely*. A new game now: no adventures you say. On the toadstool, you are only *sitting, sitting*. *That*, you say, is an adventure, Wendy. Are you, dear bird, losing *interest, interest*? I will undo a bad hem *for you*; I will roll out dough and make fresh noodles *for you*; I will nurse the fresh wound *for you*; I will remember the new adventure and later tell it *for you*. And Slightly, poor Slightly, who has been trying so very hard to be just like you—can you, do you think you can just this once *let him*? The poor boy, he can hardly take one more scolding. The babes are all bathed and powdered and smuggled up in their little beds; they're make-believing at being quiet and asleep *for you*. Because when the babes are all put to their beds, well then, the mother and the father can tell each other *stories*. Oh, Wendy, have I got a story for you!

Was there, before this one, a home like mine? How many times have the boys made a house for a girl before? I daresay, they did seem awfully adept *at it*. There must have been a home like mine somewhere permanently now fixed in a photograph—its old ghost bricks somehow haunting here, a certain smell of rot climbing the

---

The Home Under Ground

There is nothing at all about this that is *haunting*. The toy goat will, however, *come alive*. But that should not be so terribly *haunting*. That anything at all should *come alive* should be *haunting*. It is a wicked thing, a very wicked thing to think: someone up there scaring us all and all of the time, too. Don't quite give up just now: you see, this is the part that ought to be *easy*.

trellis. Old skins, old skins: which one do you have the mind to try? On? How they hang like nightgowns on the clothesline. Was there, before this one, a hole like mine? How many times have you made your home in a girl before? I daresay, you did seem awfully adept *at it*. There must have been a something like mine somewhere. She too in a locket I'm sure to dig up. Old skins, old skins: which one Peter do you have the mind to try? My old nightgown: my old nightgown once held. You.

Were you locked out? *Quite* locked out? From eggshell camp to mother to the gardens—none of the birds quite *wanting you*. And will you survive quite narrowly because of the sleeve of your nursery night gown? I've a hunch, Peter; I've a hunch that you're so forgetful simply because you're so old. Grandpa was that way, too, always calling me by mother's name, just like you. The story, the story that will *make you* remember—shall I, shall I tell it to you? (Peter, I just have to say that I don't know really if any of this is *any good*.) And if I had grown to be more petite, would it have been

---

The Home Under Ground

It's only a matter of making it *come out*, into *being*. And if you don't like it, if you don't like it then, why then you just put a little shroud on it, bury it, and in a few days, it will pop out all new and naked again. That is one way you can care for babies, if you don't know how. I complain of Peter who has *buried me*. There is something oh-so-ghostly about this way of loving, don't you think? Let us pretend it is the end, already? Why, the muffins have hardly been in for ten seconds. Or has it been? Minutes? I hardly know anything much about all of that passing and passage now. Oh, Wendy! They've been in for days and days and days: count your peas, count them, count them.

possible to have easily tricked you into thinking that I *could still?* Oh dear, the kite tail isn't quite long enough; these limbs don't quite curl into the nest just right anymore; and hollow tree to the home under ground—even, even if I suck it in. Oh, dear, *perambulator*: they make it sound as if it's a machine, as if something in there is *happening*—darling baby needs to *perambulate*. Darling chickens, count your chickens. How dare they take? I'd rather keep my little Peter egg here. And which hen am I? And how many did you take?

But that question on a rather sweet subject *has been spoken*. Prior to having vanished to Neverland, our Betwixt-and-Between resided in Kensington Gardens and loved, quite deeply, a girl by the name of Maimie Mannering. It was she that he indeed asked to marry. He wanted her to *teach him* how to be afraid, how to thimble, how to play. They will love you, says Peter; they will, like me, love you; you're like a bird's nest, and oh how I do love to stroke the fur on your pelisse, Maimie; he thimbled her all the way.

The Maimie girl was wicked, quite wicked. It was a wicked thing of her to do what she did in the dark. To her brother: *Oh, look at it, Tony! It is feeling your bed with its horns—it is boring for you, O Tony, oh!* To keep her quite alive, a night-light is put in; a saucer is

---

The Home Under Ground

You've gone and forgotten all about your muffins, and you'll now make excuses and say well then they were only make-believe, but we all know better: a fire and smoke that's been here for days and days. See, little Michael here has got the black lung. Old Tinker: her wings all soiled and singed. Tootles with a mess of burnt knees. Charcoal in Slightly's hair; ashes everywhere. You see what comes, Wendy, from your make-believe?

put in; chimney smoke is put in; a scraper and door-mat and a door handle are put in; hot and cold are put in; and lastly, quite lastly, the forcing-houses are put in. So that in less than five minutes.

Funny that you should have *forgotten* how to read, says Wendy. I am certain that I have heard stories about a certain someone who used to leave you treats along with letters detailing *how to use them*. And where, just where, have you? Put your goat? The one that *she* gave you? Is it true? Is it true that it's only because? She does, yes, Wendy, remind. Me of you. I meant the reverse; I go that way. Sometimes. You must know that it is because of the island.

Who first had the fur? Collar? Pelisse? Can't we just pretend? Can't we just pretend that everything is new and for the first time first? And really now: why *get married* when you can have so many, so many? (You can *choose*!) You can't sleep here anymore; it's really

---

The Home Under Ground

It must be way past spring: the marigolds now at the peak of their *blooming*. And still, and still, he has yet to come. For me. Perhaps he has found already another *leading lady*. Yes, I do believe. And how will you say this line here? Will you, will you put some tears in it? Oh, Peter, oh Peter, darling? Has someone else, so suddenly, become a servant for you? Let you tie her up so that the tying leaves marks that can only mean she's been with you? It was quite erotic, no? You, me, some twine, the totem pole. Something now telling me that with Tiger Lily it's all been done *before*. The rose blooms: already gone. To seed. To seed. And still, you have not come. For me. Who among us will live forever? Certainly not. Certainly not me. In Kensington Gardens, another dead babe, and no Peter goat and no fairies. From this side of the window, I can see how your world looks so bright, so bright.

throwing off everything. I know a certain sheep who shan't like to be sheared. Anymore. It quite rightly will sulk into hiding when it sees those shearing scissors criss-crossing. Night now for me like that, too. (I know what you're thinking: which child will you now steal to make your next book quite right?) *"I do wish you would teach me how to be afraid, Maimie,"* he said. Maimie? asks Wendy. Who is Maimie? Never mind all of that now: your chest cold is a-clanking. It's a real one: Tiger Lily gave it me.

I say, Peter, I should like to return to a scene that is more *domestic*—no more of this highfalutin hand-of-the-creator thing. I don't quite like him, shouldn't like to meet him. And besides, I'm not quite so sure I like the way he *looks* at me. I'm sorry for the burnt biscuits, the blackened oven, the charred bird; it's just that I know how quickly you run to smoke when you see Tiger Lily's. I should like some berry juice, too, you know. You know. You shouldn't keep on smashing it up just *for her*. She's plenty of braves to be making juice for. Something quite strange, Peter: how you put it in. I complain of Peter, who doesn't quite know *how to put it in*. He *didn't even*

The Home Under Ground

Shoreline forgets; marauders forget; empty vial forgets; old crocodile—he *never* forgets; clamshell forgets; old spoon forgets; seasons forget; old lilac bloom all gone to seed now and forgets; even the fat storm-cloud gets so lazy with forgetting and forgets; old bedroom forgets—forgets to be what it ought to be (where's the roses all trellising up and the babes peeping in, peeping in?); old bones never forget; old shadow *never forgets*—wants to *go back, go back*; space there between two stars never forgets—wants to swallow you, whole and forever, won't let you ever *go back, go back.*

know how a father does till I showed him. And now you've gone and put too much frosting on your cinnamon bun. But which one *are you?* says he.

Let us start a Daily Gazette, says she, so that we'll be able to archive all of our adventures. Good idea. Good idea. But say, Wendy, none of us on the island have ever learned *to read*, excepting Hook, and well then, he'll know all of our secrets and what then? For Peter, however, it has little to do with Hook and more to do with the dreams of the future generations of children who may know too much about what the island brings. I say, Wendy, you shan't write; you shan't write a thing. We shall just carry on *like this*—with a storytelling of things that *may* or *may not* be.

What then will you do to lure me when I have already figured out that those things with which you brought me here turned out to be your playthings: the fairies, the papoose, the mermaids, why, even the mother of the whelpings. *My* pet wolf! Indeed. Will you then invent another *girlthing*? Perhaps you'll say *ponies*, but that's terribly old-fashioned now, little birdie. Girls now, well, we'd like something a bit more *flashy*.

The Home Under Ground

Peter, Peter, my bed here is *sinking*, and the kite isn't coming. I daresay it *isn't coming*. Will I too shine so bright and suddenly and urge you, urge you on and in? Will you, even though I'm quite so grown, take me still part of the way? But then, what then? I didn't quite expect that the story would end. This way. Who now is brushing the brambles from your hair and boy skin? Who now administers your medicine? Who now is dressing your wounds, attending to your scabs, forgiving your sins? Does she, like me, cherish each and every little pea?

Old parrot now repeating. Things I've said. It'll circle the island bringing news, bringing news of who's dying, who's dead. I don't like that thing—barking all day. If you don't like something, Wendy, just kill it. If you kill it, it won't bother you anymore, and then you'll be able to write without all of that terrible noise and disturbance. But what if I try to kill it and it doesn't die and it just flies back to Hook and speaks of the terrible thing that I have just done? But which is worse, Wendy, that or having it tell the whole of the island how you took turns with braves, all of them, one by one? I only went, she said; I only went to tell them to stop calling me a squaw. Of course, Wendy; oh, but, yes, that *is* old news by now; I do say that is quite *old* news now: Tiger Lily howled of it all night; Tiger Lily swore vengeance. But will we know, Wendy? Will we know when the baby is born, which one it belongs to? Big storm cloud coming in from the West, all spectacular and island bound. The

---

The Home Under Ground

Perhaps kite *forgets*. After all, even mothers *forget*; little girls *forget*; Peter, too, *forgets*. That's the way it will end: it will end simply because someone *forgets*—especially now that we're forbidden to write anything down. There's a bird living in the eaves; I hadn't before noticed. It doesn't sing—not even one pretty song for me. Maybe it has forgotten the songs, or maybe, better yet, maybe it's a little boy who scratched too much where it itched, and the bristling feathers done come and come. You, too, Wendy, don't forget: you too were once a little bird, but by now you've quite *forgotten* everything about that. How many eggs do you think this here basket *will hold*? A dozen, surely. Surely. But maybe, maybe not. I hardly know: how much weighs an egg? I'm much heavier these days, I do think—not so light anymore. Perhaps the kite, even if it did remember, could not carry me away anyway.

rain will put the Hook in a frenzy; onboard, it will make slip little feet. Or maybe this will be the perfect night for them to bury the booty, to rid the ship of its *evidence*.

Peter, you must know. You must know that I loved you only and most of all and that is why I laid out the milk and the cheese-cakes and the butter and honey and complained that the braves had been referring to me as a squaw. I suppose; I suppose that on most days I am *happy*; it's just on those nights when you have only given me make-believe tea and then I don't see you again for days that I want to go. And because there really is no place to go, I go to Hook who knows how to *tickle* things. You see: there's a smile on my face before long! And besides: he's real apples, real figs, real plums. He'll make me a little doll with a corn cob, a little Johnny cake with sugar and meal, and he'll even take my measurements so that I will fit even though I might have grown. He doesn't even mind a little bit of blood. The moon, all *sassy* now.

Don't you think this little exchange here is *getting old*? I complain of this exchange, Tootles says, which is getting quite old. Let us take a survey then and see just how we can continue on here without

---

The Home Under Ground

I think it's about time that we've let these things *go* now. Tulips all gone to wilt now. Porcupine done gone to sleep now—that's one animal that's definitely *not* funny, not funny at all. Have you a *hole?* In your pocket? See, I'll take out my housewife and make it all better. Do you get a certain strangling sensation upon seeing this box? It's merely a *house-wife*, that's all. But it's about time, I think, that we've let these things go now. Little house all dusty and crumbling now. Fake roses all a-dying.

having to reinvent too much. Or, better yet, let's take a test and ascertain just what has transpired so that we can make it all new again. True or False: When I arrived here, I had gray in my hair. Question 2 (fill in the blank): The Never bird saved Peter with her _____. Quite unfair. Quite unfair, Wendy, to the Peter bird—he's so old and senile. You know he won't remember a thing. You know this about him, lady! Why do you insist on making him remember that you two did it? I think he's quite over *that* now. Of course, you are quite nice; of course, you are loving; why then some days do you wake up with so much venom? I do say, Wendy, it is not ladylike, you know. It isn't like a mother should. I say that you make it up; I say that you make us pancakes.

Hook pricks all over my spine I've. I'll stay in bed and complain of a *sickness*; if asked, I'll say that the Tinker Bell has *done this*. She did it out of jealously. Maybe he'll think I'm gravely ill, that another thimble will save. Me.

Maybe she's too obsessed with something else to make the story what it should be. Why, yes, Tootles, I have noticed that lately,

---

The Home Under Ground

Winter coming now. And have you bearsuits for me and John and baby Michael? Are there even any baby bears *left* to kill? Oh, bears gone into their sleeping caves by now. They might have come, I think, to eat us anyway. Never mind that scarf, Peter; it's all full of your dead fairy folk—that's why it glistens and sparkles so, and that is how I will fly back to mother; I'll shake out little bits of fairy dust at a time until I'm quite home and will you miss me then? And will you speak on *it* then? And will you ask a certain question on a rather sweet subject *then*?

lately she's taken to spinning heaps of wool from the Never sheep. And where have they come from, come from? New sheep done sprung? And a spinning wheel too has come from out of nowhere? 'Tis were imagined, *imagined*. Why take to spinning and leave your boys, and leave your boys to play baa baa black sheep? (I do say that *something's* in the hay!) Ooh oooh oooh, says Tootles, do you think, do you think the girl Wendy is spinning us suits, new sheep suits, and we can finally change out of these here old bearsuits? Why, kill a sheep first and see if it fits, if it fits *true*, and then go and see what Peter will say to you; none of the boys, however, are quite that brave; none want to be chased out and away from the Neverland because *chasing* quite means a *disappearance*. Happened once to an old Never monarch; old butterfly never quite said the right words to the Peter bird, who quite made the thing disappear simply.

The Home Under Ground

Hollyhocks blooming all up the side of the trellis, so heavy they need to be tied back lest they droop and break. Neverland earth so rich it will grow anything. Out to the heavens. And so I hold so tightly my little bean lest it escape, implant itself, and fly away from me. Something sinister washed up on the seashore saying *too late, too late*. What is a girl to do? One who is a very little one? Maybe a doctor, a *real* doctor, will come? Will come? Old Hook: all lying with *his* black bag and stethoscope: no real thermometer *in there*. I say, Hook, I say, I do think I'm coming down with *something*. A little bird; a little bird. Do you think that *for this* it's possible for you to bake me a little cake? Or does it not work that way? Tell me: how do you tell time when your instruments, your landscape keeps changing? The astrolabe says something in conflict with the stars.

Ooooohhhh, oooohhh, get this, get this, Tootles says, I asked her, and she says that she quite intends, she quite intends to stay on *through the winter* and to the spring, and that is why, that is why she's a-spinning a Never cloak to wear for then, to meet the cold. We've bearsuits; she does not; the Wendy bird will freeze, will freeze, and her Never house all slatty. And what has she in her spinning basket there? Oh, mermaids' hair, butterfly wings, locks of Hook's hair, pixie dust, dead pixies' wings, a myriad of sparkling things, a few stars here, a few Never leaves there; she's spinning them *right in*; I daresay she'll blend in and then what then? Will the Peter bird still *love her*? Because, as you know, he only loves them when they are quite *different*. But, Tootles, she will still have *that thing*. What thing? What thing? I hardly know what you mean by *that thing*. I complain of Wendy who has gone nights now without telling us a story. Wendy, she's in to her elbows in the wash basin trying to demusk the sheep fleece. It's a ram, you see, and it has a certain *aroma*; it's ever-so-much stronger than you might think.

The *business* trip will take eleven days; will you be quite lonesome without. Me? The doves all crying; why, yes, you've guessed it, Wendy! In the eaves. Don't be. So sad. Isn't this exactly the kind

---

The Home Under Ground

Wendy, have you quite come to terms with what it means to *fly home?* I don't quite think so; you see, I've a certain crick in my neck from all of that spinning, and the applying of various poultices—Tiger Lily's pussy lard and Peter's toe jam—haven't quite been working, although Tiger Lily's father quite said they would. So, no, I haven't actually been thinking too much on what it means to *fly home*. Why don't you tell me.

of life you imagined. For me? Oh, no. Oh, no. There will be no lovenotes sent to you in starcode; the boss simply won't allow. It. If you like, maybe you could leave. A note with the secretary. She'll be happy. To help. You. This, I know. For certain. She's always so eager. To please. But you mustn't. Cry, Wendy. That won't do; that won't do. At all. Oh, there! Will you look at. The time. It's about time, really. It's about time that. I got going. And what's that, you say? The cradle? We'll discuss it. Later. When I get back. Home. Isn't it a wonder? Really. That belly of yours is really. A wonder. Quite.

The look in his eyes: it is *delicious*. His eyes say that he'd like to shred Hook to pieces with his good sword, the sword that cut Hook's hand off, and not his hobby one. But sometimes he'll mistake the good sword for the hobby sword: this can make a meeting with anything quite *dangerous*. For him, it isn't a matter of *unknowing* but rather a matter of *forgetting*. Peter is the boy of *forgetting*. (Wendy would like to *forget* that.) Well, aren't *you* clever; aren't you *just the part*! For he is *just the part*, you know. That's her! That's *my* Wendy, he'll say when he sees *just the right girl*. (The prop is only make-believe!) She *is* just the right girl. Oh, but won't the *real* old lady

---

The Home Under Ground

Wendy, I daresay I think it's about time that we let these things *go* now. Wolf has stopped crying; little lost egg yolk has stopped crying; centipede and caterpillar have stopped crying; old Smee, he of the lost marbles, even he, Wendy, has stopped crying. Old kite all tattered and soiled now—even it has stopped crying. It's only you now who won't stop. Crying. Good god, old lady, you must stop crying. See, see that old moon: close one eye and then two fists over between those two stars there: there you will fly.

be quite jealous? Won't she just get all Tinker Bell on us? Start pricking and plotting some sort of death for the girl? Won't matter; won't matter: something will *save* her; something always *saves* her. That's how the story always ends. Nothing really happens when the Tinker Bell tries to kill anyone. Nor crocs; nor bearded men. Just the Peter bird, then? Just the Peter bird then.

Is it real, Peter, is it real that you have *left me*? I complain of Peter, who has *left me*. The leaving was not so make-believe. I too, like Tink, will spend the rest of the whole of my life glorying in being. Abandoned. Tink says she *glories in being abandoned*.

Not so much as a sorry-to-lose-you between them! If she did not mind the parting, he was going to show her, was Peter, that neither did he. But of course he cared very much. Or so, that is the story that we tell ourselves, the story we *want* to believe. But doesn't caring *very much* mean *everything*? As in: I'd do *anything*? No, we hadn't thought so;

The Home Under Ground

Maybe everything's just falling apart now: skeleton leaves showing their seams. I know how this will go: you'll say that you don't really *love* me. Here: take something. To remember me. By. That's the way the story goes, right, Peter bird? And will you come for any *gifts*? I do fear that I've quite run dry of *stories*. You've heard them all before. Oh, yes, but you do forget. You'll forget this one too I guess. No amount of reminding will get you to think of this one in a year's time. Or maybe. Maybe if I can teach the Never birds to say my name. Maybe if I can get one of the Never boys to keep reminding—oh, but they die. They die, too. They die from the cuts and scrapes from wars with the braves with the wolves with the grizzlies with the pirates too, and you'll *replace*. Them. That, you'll do. As is your fashion. And you'll replace me, too. Replace; replace; replace. It's such a *funny* word: replace.

we thought not. But oh, Wendy, is that there your manuscript all caught in the trees? Did the Peter bird get angry and wish it gone and it got all caught up in the branches there? There *will* be a story for you to leave, but your leaving will insist on it more that you. What's that you say? You have a little papoose? A little cocoon to hang, too? Mother wolf all dead now: will your little whelps be going, too? Will they need a nursery room? Shall we, Wendy? Shall we turn your house into a whelp rumpus room?

See, Wendy, he doesn't want to *have* the cake; he wants to *eat* it; that is what makes him just like every other little bird. If you save the cake, well, it gets old anyhow anyway, and no one wants it then; no fighting over it then; cake doesn't get eaten so cake's all sad and lonesome now; that's what happens when a cake gets old; gets old. But didn't the little man say that I should look lovely, lovely at sixty-six and that we should hurry up to get there to see, to see if anything about me had *changed?* I daresay, I already need to stitch my shadow in a bit more tightly here and there. There's some red spilling out already. Already? Already: is that always to mean *too soon?* I complain of *already* who's making it happen. Too soon.

The Home Under Ground

The grown-ups again have *spoilt* everything. They too will take the Wendy girl away. Peter didn't leave the room, and that is why it happened this way. If only he didn't stay. But he did, and he told *his* story. And it was his story that made it so that the girl Wendy wished to go away. You see, it is *story* that takes them. The *dread* is what makes Wendy *forgetful: Peter, will you make the necessary arrangements?* It's quite like a funeral. This is what happens when Peter doesn't forget. And oh don't you wish he hadn't?

Old story: Tootles after his first days on the island: I'm so *sorry*, Peter: I haven't quite figured out just how it is that I might take a Never poo. Sometimes, you see, when I've been telling you that it's pretend time to go to the bathroom, I've had some BMs that were not quite make-believe and not knowing just how to go about disposing, I've been lugging them to the mermaids' lagoon. I said, look here, these are brownies that Peter made for you. At first, they seemed quite happy, but lately, they seem quite sick with vomiting, with something like the influenza, and that is the only reason why I come to you to ask how to properly dispose of Never poo. He tells this story to Wendy; he's the one ordered by Peter to daily empty out Wendy's Never loo.

Tell me, Peter: why didn't we have a Never camera so that I might take home with me a negative of you? Something that I could always let the light shine through. An inverse image of you. And you're (sic) little baby teeth: *quite* bewitching! That is so attractive

---

The Home Under Ground

We could, you know, wait. We could wait to see if Maimie leaves a toy wolf out in the secret spot in the Gardens. Nibs: Maimie all dead now. No one else quite *replaced* to leave toys in the Gardens. That's why we steal real boys, real food, real hens, real goats, real eggs. Where have the bearsuits come from then? Why, we killed bears, Peter; you told us to do so. So much bloodshed, you know. Quite a few *adventures*, you know. Pirates *quite real*; planks *quite real*; sharks down there *quite real*; all this hovering in the in-between—that's *quite real* too I do believe, excepting perhaps for you, a Betwixt-and-Between. And what if the wolf wasn't a mother, wasn't a mother at all? What then? Fathers are ferocious, Peter—that you know.

of you. And, why, today, how charming: you're all full of seaweed: even your teeth, as if you've been munching on the lip of the lagoon. A guppy all coiled in your ear; a sand crab in your belly hole. I do say: maybe there's a sea worm, somewhere, up you. Can you resist? Can you resist, Peter? They're lulling at the moon: you should be lulling, too, at the moon. And that's how you come to be. This way. Give yourself one more thing to blame *it* on.

Seasonal change: a bit more bitterness in the tart, in the dark, in the pineapple upside down; more crisp in the apple crisp, in the dusk, in the unlayering leaves. But there's more to it, to this story than the Peter bird will let on. For once now, for once now, the rain has let up. If there hadn't been a mother Wendy, why, they would have been out in it for days, days. And Peter would have lost some boys to the sickness of rain and would have been so lonely then. He would have buried them out in the grove of lilacs—down low where so many blackberries grow. This is an *addition* that some mother or other made long ago. Is it that you retell a story to make it. *True?* I complain then of the storyteller who retells a story to make it true. The story to be retold is the story of how Peter and Wendy were marooned. That one didn't quite go as it should: mermaid girl all frolicking off in the waters there, and when he sees the big kite

The Home Under Ground

Are you quite sure that the window will be *left open*? How can you be so sure, Wendy? What if mother got so tired with the waiting that she went and found other birds? After all, she so did love to be. A mother. Maybe we shouldn't think so hard or anymore and just let what happens happens. We can *come back*, can't we, Peter?

a-coming, Peter says to Wendy, go, go, go! Or maybe it shouldn't happen quite like that.

Remember always: that *look* in his eyes. That look is the look that means he cares not if his sword is real or make-believe: he only has it in mind *to kill*. That is what that look means. You'll see it surely if you haven't until now. It's the same look that means that he doesn't know you, at least not *right now*. He will fly on maybe without you. *I say, Wendy, always if you see me forgetting you, just keep on saying 'I'm Wendy,' and then I'll remember.* But will it work *always?* I say, Peter, always if you see me wanting you…what then? For now: peaches; for now:

Mother *moves away*, Peter, and all the little baby birds fly, too. It's nothing *personal*; it's just that the husband just thinks that maybe perhaps you've had your last trouncing about. Why, you know, a *future* husband. We see him on the train platform; he's there to meet a woman of ever-so-uncertain age. You're so fond of writing about things that happen in the future; you should know what by this I mean. Island all a bit too pew-y now, too quiet now. No matter what,

---

The Home Under Ground

Mother wolf all dead now. Do you think we were just a bit too late to be with her during her dying? During her last days? Oh my! She was all confused, says whelp four. Whelp two died, too, and Peter not in time for that either. It was just the way it *happened*. So strange. So strange. He even rushed out of the clouds so that he might be there *in time*. Poor mother wolf: perhaps it is better for her; she never did quite get over the death of wolf one: wolf one all a vague whistling the whole of the rest of her life.

Peter, baby swans follow their mother; see: just like that constellation in the stars. Your soup: all a-brimming, swan flesh and stars, and it's all make-believe.

The rope marks will not *disappear*. Oh, happier days, when Peter was just a dream that 'came more and more. Real. I have hurt myself, she says, falling. That is the story she tells Peter to get Peter to forget about lovers. Are you so surprised, Wendy, that I should now come for you? Flowers are still, still in bloom, even this late, in bloom; how far, how long does it take for the heart to grow fond, fonder still? You see, I break things up *here* while you're still the girl Wendy to spare us, spare us. Is that copper? Has it turned all green and pretty? Why, yes, Wendy, it was new and shiny when you first gave it to me.

Yes, it is a dull beginning. I say, let us pretend that it is the end. But how should it be, the end? You see, Peter, I too, alone, without you, can have *adventures*. And that is why I now must go. I can leave *you*. Imagine that! Bet you didn't quite think. Of that. And I will take all my stories, the children, and half the furniture, too. But I didn't quite want to leave, like that. I should like to spend some

---

The Home Under Ground

Old fat cloud shunt up against the moon now. Lay on your back, Wendy; like this, and see now you can sleep. This layer of cloud: a little less *turbulent*. I don't quite think I like where it is that you are taking me. After all: there were *preparations* made. I don't think I like to go where there have been *preparations*. I haven't quite been *prepared* for the. Is it because your water gourd is breaking? Old umbilical vine twisting towards where we are going.

time with my pumpkins, with my roses, too. Will everything be just like this, just like this when I return to you? Please don't say that there should be another girl sleeping. In my bed. Why look, Peter. You can, without me, *entertain*. Why, look at your Neverland silver, your single-serving spoon.

Mummy and daddy will take us. I am sure they will take the whole lot of us. They've a house *full* of *nurseries*, and if it isn't enough, why, they'll move from 27 to a completely different house, a house far out in the country, so far that the old man of the stories cannot come out to visit us. That's the way maybe that it should be, maybe. Old Nana anyway wants to run, to run. She'll die soon anyway, and she, too, will be *replaced, replaced*. How is *that* for a *story*? Mummy and daddy will *take* us; I'm sure they will take the whole lot of us. Why, and if they haven't enough nurseries, we'll transform the parlor into one

---

The Home Under Ground

Peter, Peter: you're quite the *grave digger*. The babes newly planted here by you, all mossed over by now with tombstones, too. And when I die, will you, will you dig a grave for me? Or will I be just too big, too ordinary? I should require a bit more digging, you know. The ground now so terribly shattering. Perhaps it is better to go out the way of the pirates: something certain and sinister anyway about their ship: all a dead black bird; the sails all a crushed bird wing. I should require a bit more *digging*. In the case of the love story here inserted: certainly a bit more digging. I, too, shall be *a ghost*: I think; I know; I connote. The Never locust: all wedged into a bale of hay. And where has this wheat field come from? Suddenly, a wheat field just sprung, just sprung: a new life. Cross it, Wendy, and you shall see. See how the twilight catches the grains: so sparkly. Here: I'll walk with you, but only part of the way. But I want to go all the way with you, Peter: all the way.

and move beds in there and everything. And to think! To think that when you've grown, you can have a job that you go to by railway. There's no railway in this here Never. And, well, quite simply: aren't you weary of going about with bare feet? How is *this* for an ending? I complain of Wendy, says Tootles; I complain of Wendy, who is always wanting to give us endings.

Perhaps we will save *that* for the very, very end. *That* should be reserved for the very end. A storyteller knows that. Knows that much, at least. Illuminate then the earthbound tree; Mr. Caw all taking attendance there. Are all the children accounted for, accounted for? Only one of us knows how to perch right, just so. Peter's talons can quite curl around the bark. Will you, Wendy, will you remain with me? Mr. Caw can make it so that you have special claws, special wings. And don't you want wings, Wendy? I should think you would. Want wings. See: there's an *itching*; an itching.

The Home Under Ground

Poor old pussycat: you'll live out your life on the plank forever. Maybe ole Smee will throw you the remains of some fish or other. Poor old pussycat: you've been chased out of the pantry. Old geese, you won't chase them down, just yet, just yet; those there *can fly*; they're the *wild* kind, but not those; those have been *domesticated*. And, you, too, like the Peter bird, somewhat feral, a Betwixt-and-Between: that is why you aren't being pet, you know. No one wants to love forever a wild thing. We know just what happens when you get bored and weary: there will be a late night; there will be a *mystery*. That is why you have dreams of the jungle, dear pussy. Dear pussy, the big cats will come soon; they'll take on you.

See: it's ever so much more interesting with real-life encroaching. That's the small and the short of it. Oh, I see: I see: the Joke's on *me*: it is indeed Lock Out time: Lock Out time for the girl Wendy. Should she be barred now from the Neverland, and why? The hem not quite, not quite reaching, reaching? (Oh, that *old* story.) If only she had been the girl with the fur pelisse then. Then. Maybe there would have been a bit of her the Peter bird would have liked, stroking; maybe she would have been loved because she was *like* a nest. And don't you look exactly, I mean *exactly* like a nest? Mr. Caw so big: he takes up the whole of the tree; a black wing taking up the whole of the sky, the late-summer scene: maybe he's all just shadow now, a big black mashed feather of a thing; I daresay it makes me miss a certain somebody. And will you, too, Mr., buy me a dog? Buy me a dog to make me less *lonely*? And then will you take the dog

---

The Home Under Ground

And have the nightmares started, started? Ole Hook by the curtains, parting, parting. No, that's Peter, not Hook: Peter who loves the parting, parting. At night, balled up and crying: oh, Peter, did you dream, did you dream of your mother? And was it a beautiful dream? Vengeance all lapped up in the clouds now; a sickle chamber come to greet me; was it true that mailboxes would be *this empty?*; no one warned of *that*; nightmares sometimes make me want to *go back, go back*; stars all sinister; night-light all sinister; doggie nurse all *sinister*; peeing all sinister; (can't help but think—can't help but think that I am quite done with the peeing); underbelly of toads so sinister; Jolly Roger hull so sinister. Oh, dear Peter, you didn't tell me right away that you were a gravedigger. My goodness, my goodness, and your home *is* under ground. Have we quite reached the end yet? Or is there still that one story to tell? Tell it, Wendy; tell it.

to gather, to gather. Your lost boys all a-trouncing after *my* dog. I suppose that's how they live in houses above ground. I daresay I'd rather be below.

To guide her strange craft: that is what the girl Wendy needs to do in order reach safety, if she. Wanted to, which she doesn't, you see. Ever so much more *adventurous* now on the island made real, made real. Hook: whatever transpired here between us should be kept between you and me, you and me. But the apples, the apples *were* delicious. Old sea cat: lured me, *lured* me. For you: I give a lock of Wendy hair. For you: I set off future distress flares: cometome-cometomecometome. *I'm Wendy.* There was so much nice rocking in that Jolly brig there. Darling: avast.

Mermaids: all deserted *now*; hair all wrapped up in algae. They're only *playing* dead, the Peter bird says, because they think you've come to get 'em. Some little bird told 'em so—told 'em that you were

---

The Home Under Ground

We are on something, Wendy, and it's growing *smaller* and *smaller*; that is *why*, Wendy. The island's made real, and so is the small thing that's growing smaller. Stand on the smallest part of it on tiptoe and still, the thing will happen, and that is why the mermaids are here to sing; they know when the small thing happens, when the moon needs singing to. Old turtle lived two hundred years, went belly up there, and the mermaids took to calling to the moon then, too. If you feel ever so many *shudders*, Wendy, I will only feel *just the one*. See: something is *engulfing*. It is growing smaller and smaller, Peter, because, I do believe it's because of me: the girl Wendy growing *bigger* and *bigger*: so big. So big that baby's kite I fear won't anymore save me. It is *engulfing*; it is.

out to get 'em. That is what love *can do*: it can make you go out and get 'em.

And have you already found another little girl to? Until, until. Should I speed up the birth and delivery in order to see you, see you?

Crocodile come now, and you have killed. My love. Where is it that I should go? Perhaps, perhaps I'll say that it's time, boys: it's about that time that we went to go see mother. (We'll see what look the Peter bird has in his eyes then.) Jars of preserves done gone empty: Tootles been eating; face and hands all slimy. He's the one who always seems to be *in trouble*. What have we here, Peter? Have I not left you enough varieties of: maple, boysenberry, lingonberry, raspberry, blueberry, lemon, apple, cherry. Not enough? Not enough *variety* for you? But doesn't the coffee taste *good* this

---

The Home Under Ground

To guide her strange craft (83): that is what the Never bird needs to do in order to save the Peter bird from drowning; all the lessons from the swans, the chickadees, the swallows, the whip-poor-wills too could not teach the Betwixt-and-Between to keep from drowning. (That is what we learned when we heard about the girl Maimie. Why, Peter, you never mentioned *her* before, says Wendy.) Should the rock symbolize whence hope springs? New lives already done sprung, done sprung; new lives, new lives always messing up everything: that Never boy and that Never boy and that Never boy all too big for their knickerbottoms and now what and what then? And shall we? Shall we try to *play* again? Oh, no! Oh, no! dear man: you see: we are seriously struggling to make an *ending* happen. Here. Ole twins are readying for school now: lunch pail all duly packed by mother now. Fine: go on then: walk along the platform and see: see how all of this for *you* will end.

morning? Coffee: drink it; that's what grown-ups *do*. They do. You shan't have *this* jam; this jam's no longer *for you*. Love all killed now, and the children hated him, didn't they? They booed; they *frowned*. And I bet, I bet, all the little girls threw thimbles at you. Oh, Peter, you're turning every pocket, *every* pocket: inside out, inside out! But I have the *acorn button*. The acorn button is something that, up until now, I've kept. Silent about.

Children have the strangest adventures without being troubled by them. For instance, they may remember to mention, a week after the event happened, that when they were in the wood they met their dead father and had a game with him. But maybe, Wendy, maybe you'd like to *see me* one last time, one last time. But I shouldn't like to cause any *trouble* for you or your husband or your brood. If you think it would, that is, cause *trouble*, well then, well then. (Such a long fortnight in Paris with you!) And he's such a *good* husband, too: see how much he *loves*, how much he *dotes* on you. He keeps the stove all lit and warm *for you*. He puts a baby in the cradle *for you*. He signs the greeting cards together *with you*. That's a good husband,

---

The Home Under Ground

Wendy began to be scrawled all over with him. As you will; as you will: read this *as you will*. Whether the he is the little Betwixt-and-Between or whether the Betwixt-and-Between is he: there is a male hand, and it is *scrawling* on a little girl. All over, that is. At what point is the girl no longer herself but a mere *scrawling*? Scrawling, Wendy, I daresay, in this light, in this light, I could scrawl you all day. Have we really passed the day in scrawling? Yes, Peter: we have scrawled, and that is why I have an acorn button from you, from you.

Wendy, an ever-so-good one that is he. I have a new nest here; I've put it together *so nicely*; I would like to show you, but not if you think it would cause. Trouble. But shouldn't there be, at a last meeting, *something said?* Should I say a little something sweet and true *for you*, Wendy, *for you?* I missed the marrying, didn't want to be a man for you; that I would never do; not even *for you*, Wendy, and how ever-so-much I loved you. I loved. You. You of the acorn caps; you of the precious peas. And see: my clothes still need pressing: no one does it quite like you, quite loved me like you. Teeth all yellowed now; gum line all receding; hair all thinning now; and no children to remind me. I suppose I was always so old and diseased and yet still, Wendy, you *loved me.* You loved me with the holes in my socks, holes in my knees. I fly over your house, Wendy, over and over and I think to see you, but I never do see. You. Would you like to see my new little nest? I shouldn't like to cause any *trouble* for you and Mr. But, Peter, if I decline such a request, wouldn't it show, wouldn't it show that I had a little something *withheld?* That there was a reason why, still, I should not see you? And what has any of

---

The Home Under Ground

The Peter is so terribly upset: no one will stop calling him. Pan. That's not who he is, you know. Why look: he works in an office and wears a tie too and on occasion, why, yes, he has had a beard even. Do you think it's because some girl somewhere left the toy train out in the night for the Peter and it entered the Never world? That may have been one story. About how it *happened*. It *happened*; that's for sure. The Mrs. quite upset. The sky all a loam of engine smoke. Which grave marker had he? PP. The headlines will read. They will read, and that's how we will know that the PP has.

this to do with the *opening?* Why, because you see, I had seen you, I had been seeing you: in dreams, in flashes, in the in-between.

But in her dream he had rent the film that obscures the Neverland. And that is what made the girl Wendy *different* from the other girl children; Wendy had been *courted* by the Peter bird. In *her* dream he had rent the film, and that is how they should have known that Peter was coming for them. She thinks: this is why I am ever so better than Maimie: *he* came for *me*: I just didn't lose myself there; this must mean that maybe perhaps he loves me. Quite, ever so much more than Maimie. And besides, what kind of name anyhow is Maimie? Better to have a name that came from not being able to say it properly. I'm Wendy.

Tinker Bell: she's mending all the *pots and kettles.* Pots and kettles, wouldn't you know it, need *a lot,* quite a lot of mending. Why, isn't it a task just a bit too big for a fairy? How many kettles have you, have you anyhow in the Neverland? I daresay, whatever for do you need so many kettles? Tinker Bell: she's *hardly* dressed you know. That seems to be the way it is with the Never womenfolk: there's hardly a leaf there to shelter the little tuft of pubis-a-wisp. (It's shimmering white down there!) Tinker Bell: she has such a big

---

The Home Under Ground

Perhaps there should always be *more.* Love involved. That is what makes for a good story. Wendy, I do say that I will love you more. I just need more. Time. Cloud there in the distance all like a brig gone awry. You and I: the last survivors. For sure; for sure. Some wreck occurred here, here, here at your heart. Something in there all a mess now, I know. Surely if I play at being Never doctor. Surely.

nether eye, as if, as if she's been digging for something. (I'm not sure if we're *allowed* to say it. But isn't this adventure getting quite long, quite long now?) Tinker Bell: how go you?; how go you when the season is done? Old cicada shells all gleaming out at sea. There's a little boat for you, for you. Tinker Bell: the Never catfish would like to eat you. Do you feel rather lonely out there by yourself? I should think you would feel *rather* lonely out there. By yourself. Is it true that Peter forgot to teach you too how to stop? (I complain of Peter who didn't bother to teach us *how to stop*.) Tinker Bell: is there really a pot of gold somewhere, somewhere? I should think not. The Hook bird would like to eat you. The Smee bird, too; you see, you've the loveliest and littlest of pillows, the tiny tiny pin-prick of a pocket. And that is why, for sure, that all of the Never birds would like *to eat you*. Tinker Bell: there ought to be another scenario here *for you*. Tomorrow, we shall write it: we shall write it *true*.

There was ever such a *tiny* room for you. Little golden straws you placed all in an acorn cap, little Peter fingernail clippings glittering like half-moons. And has anyone, anyone bothered to feed you baby crabs? Why, they'd be just the right size for you! I do say, Tinker,

---

The Home Under Ground

Let us make a telegram tree, and we'll see in the morning which one of us has gotten a message. Will that do? Will that do *for you*? Who among us overnight will play at being the telegraph master? Who among us will play at being the one to hang the telegrams from trees? I say, should we go to the house? Should we go a-knocking? But that is how the grown-ups do it; we will have to do it differently from them. We'll write on the back of the skeleton leaves. Oh, dead fairy all huddled up in this one here.

that is terribly *cute*. But what have we here? What is this? Have you, Tink, have you gotten stuck with the shorter stick? The shorter end *of it?* We know you meant to kill, to kill. Peter's pubes all strung up with crustaceans and barnacles: what must be hiding deep within the lagoon, gathering itself in some fishy fallopian tube? Why, it does have fins and gills; it does look incredibly *fishlike*: what phylum is it, is it? But now, Tink, let us return to you, to you. Have you tired of the mending? I do say this hole here looks purposefully placed. Such a little hole too; do you think the Peter bird will break

---

The Home Under Ground

Little Tink: your light is quite *out*. You might have begun so *small*, so *suddenly*. Why, that lantern carried through the air: that's how you began. (Michael tells it so, and with him being baby, we let him make up the story sometimes, too. Also, it isn't quite so fair is it? It isn't quite so fair how Peter oftentimes, always gets authorship. Perhaps it's because little man loved the other boy so and didn't want to let on. Too much.) Little Tink: did you love for exactly eleven months and a day? I see, I see the little fairy baby you're carrying: crawled outside of you as a little lump of gold. Smee found it in a little cavern, filled a cavity with it: with your little baby. She's all singing in his tooth now. Tink: I knew how badly you wanted to be. With Peter. And how he locked you up on account. Of me. These things: can we say *sorry* for? I know only now that I, like you, felt the certain ache and search for something to fill, to fill: that's why you stole the peas; that's why you slept in a pod. I can only forgive you this now. I can tell you that on the day of your funeral, why, Peter looked all glazed over; maybe he had the *shakes?* He kept wanting to do *something else*. Why, I think I should like to be a farmer, says he, right when we were sending you out to sea.

through, break through? (He should be in a birdcage, not you; not you.) That is all you want, isn't it, a dear lady like you, is to have the Peter bird break through? Why, it looks as if you're limping just a bit, just a bit. Perhaps you'll need a bandage and crutches, too; where ever will we get such small medical supplies for you? The Tinker dental dam; the Tinker tampon. Old little tin cup you

---

The Home Under Ground

This much is ever so real; this much isn't make-believe: *Peter Pan can do a great deal in ten minutes.* He can do a great deal *to you.* For example, he can put a little something inside of you, and you will carry that for the rest of your life; thimble all empty underneath in the inside. The molar pregnancy: lasting, lasting; placenta all set to bursting, all full of nothing, nothing. I like the way they scurry about, the land crabs, says she. We haven't any land crabs back home. Maybe I can pluck one from the Never shore and take it, take it? Home. How long, Peter, might it take? To go all the way? With you? Is the film rent? Is the sky rent? How much longer do I have? Until? You no longer adore? Me? It never takes ten minutes to get anywhere, anywhere. And should I change my mind up on that cloud there? How would that work? Would I be able to return then, to return then to the Never nest? I should very much want to stay the whole of the rest of my life in our little Never love nest. But I do have the worms, and I do need for mother to take me to a proper doctor—everything all so much worse when you play at being. It. (Or when Jas Hook plays at being *it.*) So embarrassed now of my Never loo: worms all a-waving, all a-wriggling like Never anemones. This ending isn't quite so *elegant*; this ending will never do, never do; please tell the lady: please tell the lady to redo, *redo.* I should be in a horse and carriage; I should be carrying a bouquet for you. And I will carry a bouquet *for you.*

drank from: look! They've taken to using it as. And your little still-birth, all like a tadpole, all a-gasping in your little kettle of water.

Also he was fond of variety, and the sport that engrossed him one moment would suddenly cease to engage him, so there was always the possibility that the next time you fell he would let you go. You see, you have to do it *today.* If you *do it* today, then you'll have something *to-morrow* that you didn't have *yesterday.* That is the way the darkness works: something unknown grows a little bigger each day. How *did* he know just what to do with the goat? He read the notes from the first one who explained to him how human children play. Fear will fall upon, anon, anon. That is why the goat was used ultimately to take the dead children away. Maimie first, then John, then Jack, then Dorothy, then mummy, then Wendy too, then Jane, then Margaret, then you, too. *Ever so much more than twenty.* Even you.

The Home Under Ground

There was quite a *pull* here: little kite strings. And to think, to think: all that time that I was in bed sleeping, I could have been here with you talking, as you say, to stars. All that time. There was quite a kick here, in the hull: a little baby foot I do believe. It swims about as if, as if part mermaid. Some days: so anxious: can't quite sleep. Little night-light: doesn't quite keep the dark out of the in-between. A brig's sail all billowing out from the curtain just now. In the morning, apples will litter the ground, and it won't be because you shook them there: something else in the air severing. Someone's come and plucked off all of the gourd blossoms; just left them there to wither. Now there shan't be any pumpkin. Pumpkin: baby all curled up in you, too. And, Peter, you daresay that *you* are the *sole survivor*? I complain of Peter who claims to be the sole survivor. There indeed *were* survivors of the wrecked brig, and I, the Wendy girl, was just *one* of them.

Parting at last with mutual expressions of good-will. Only it wasn't quite like that. There was ever-so-much of something else involved: a *briefcase* that refused to be used as a *briefcase*. And what else can be found *in there?*: a calendar and ledger, papers and toothpaste. Why have you, have you got a trip *overnight?* Will good wifey be waiting, be waiting at home? I daresay that the moon isn't quite right, isn't quite romantic tonight, all tumbleweedish, all compacted loam. Tumbleweeds, all a-blowing on the Neverland vistas. Oh, go, go and play your cowboy, go and play your torturing, go and play that you're bringing Tiger Lily home. And did you quite refuse to wear your tie to eat here at the head seat? I've made herring and the dishes here are bone. I do think you would very much like to own. A home. See: the train will take you to where you need to go. No more flying. No more flying far away from home. Nary a brig, nary

---

The Home Under Ground

The night now: all a-brimming. Something frothy about the stars. Ole cold old man living somewhere here I know. That's how we'll come to understand. We'll come to understand the stars. And have you drawn your straw? Strawing place: lines so long, so long. And have you drawn your scrawl? Scrawling place: lines so long, so long. The kite has been sent here, see?: the kite has been sent here because I daresay, Wendy, the water is reaching well past your knees. This will make it so that there is *another day* for you. (The clapping will not someday right you: that is only a trick of the fairies. So *sorry* for you.) *I am old, Peter. I am ever so much more than twenty.* So don't you get up; don't you turn up the light; don't you come near. Me. *He sat down on the floor and sobbed.* That is what Betwixt-and-Betweens do. Who is the more heartbroken now you tell me. (But it was new, Wendy, when you gave it me.) Sea foam: something like the verdigris all in it.

a whalehull, just a corset, just a corset for you. It's ghastly. It's *ghastly* all right. Only someone about yeahigh will do, will do.

This is how things *ended*, you see: ever so much more differently than the endings in Wendy's stories. And have they all gone and grown up and gotten married? I daresay they've all gotten married, and there's no tincture that'll cure *that*. Never bird: she's so *done* with all that popping out of babies. I complain of the Never bird, of middle-aged ladies who are done with the popping out of babies. We need more babies; more babies means more fairies; means more Peter treats.

The Home Under Ground

And, Peter, will you put things in *little* boxes, *quite little* boxes? Every fairy ever loved all shelved now in cigar boxes, the *petite* ones in sardine tins. Old pirates throwing these things for you *out*. Have you then a little seashell or perhaps some buttercups to decorate? To *decorate* her hair? And have you a *memento*? For you know we girls just love mementoes, would love very much to have a time with the very best one. That is some sort of story, don't you know. A box inside a box inside a box: that is how the best burials go. Mrs. Darling's mouth: a burial sideshow, all the dead ones lined up in a neat row all down and down her throat: she's all squirrelly with the dead girls. Maimie, especially, all locked up in there, too. Have you a certain element of shame, of *I do*? No, I didn't think so; I didn't think you do. Every little cocoon, each little cicada casing all blistered now; little critters done moved, done moved. Hitch your dress a little higher. That I don't need to do. Anymore; anymore; old tide knows how I've now a little grown. Old melon flowers; old hothouse flowers; old trellis flowers; I think I should like roses *best* of all. And perhaps a little jar of peas, please. And didn't you know that these sands are numbered, numbered? They number you best of all.

Next morning: it may not have been your *little feet*, says Wendy, but I have seen—I have seen the imprint of your little teeth all about the dawn; there's a certain slant of bicuspid that can only be yours, Peter, yours alone. See there, in that little fracture of sky there? And the sign of incisors all gorging upon and gouging the sky as if some animal wanted to be *let*. Out. Oh, and was it *delicious*? To feast upon the sky? Oh, oh, and now the stars, too; shall a certain star, too, be my nemesis? And I should know now why it's been two weeks since you have wanted to claw. Upon me. You have found. Your clawing elsewhere. My dear, my dear pet wolf: I will tell you the difference between A and Z.

The Home Under Ground

And where have you come from, come from? If indeed you were *made before*, then when and where was it quite? I know a place where there are little snails. Out in the sunflower field, in little furrows there. New ones, it seems, each day, each day there appear. Each day, each day I cut a bit of sunflower and take it. Home. Will Peter today notice these? Out of what is something grown? A hole here, a hole there. I know a place where there are little souls; out in the sunflower field, in little furrows there; new ones, it seems, each day, each day there appear. An emptiness where a sand crab makes home; a cavern where the Never squid calls home; a vase where the flowers wilt; a dark place where new lives done grown. *Done grown!* A hole here, a hole there, and the Wendy girl is called to mend, to mend. What is a pocket but a hole? A home. For the housewife who has grown, has grown, the home is nothing but a hole. The moon tonight so full, so full of cradles outgrown.

Acknowledgments

The title of this book as well as many italicized portions are taken from J.M. Barrie's *Peter and Wendy* (Mineola: Dover, 1999). The title is excerpted from the following: *Of course she should have roused the children at once; not merely because of the unknown that was stalking toward them, but because it was no longer good for them to sleep on a rock grown chilly* (72). Other italicized portions are taken from Barrie's *Peter Pan in Kensington Gardens* (New York: Oxford UP, 1999). Some imaginings in this piece were inspired by events in Andrew Birkin's *J.M. Barrie & the Lost Boys: The Love Story that Gave Birth to Peter Pan* (New York: Clarkson N. Potter, Inc., 1979). Notes to these references, however, seem to encumber and demystify rather than enlighten the text, and I felt for this reason that endnotes should not be included.

Grateful acknowledgement is made to the following publications where excerpts from *not merely* first appeared:

Academy of American Poets (poets.org)
Black Warrior Review
Bone Bouquet
Cavalier
Dislocate
Fourth Genre
Graduate Center Advocate
Gulf Coast
Poor Claudia
Puerto del Sol
Requited
Shampoo
Tammy

About the Author

Jenny Boully is the author of *The Book of Beginnings and Endings* (Sarabande Books), *[one love affair]** (Tarpaulin Sky Press), and *The Body: An Essay* (Essay Press). She teaches nonfiction and poetry at Columbia College Chicago.

TARPAULIN SKY PRESS
Current & Forthcoming Titles

FULL-LENGTH BOOKS

Jenny Boully, [one love affair]*

Jenny Boully, *not merely because of the unknown that was stalking toward them*

Ana Božičević, *Stars of the Night Commute*

Traci O Connor, *Recipes for Endangered Species*

Mark Cunningham, *Body Language*

Danielle Dutton, *Attempts at a Life*

Sarah Goldstein, *Fables*

Johannes Göransson, *Entrance to a colonial pageant in which we all begin to intricate*

Noah Eli Gordon & Joshua Marie Wilkinson, *Figures for a Darkroom Voice*

Gordon Massman, *The Essential Numbers 1991 - 2008*

Joyelle McSweeney, *Nylund, The Sarcographer*

Joyelle McSweeney, *Salamandrine: 8 Gothics*

Joanna Ruocco, *Man's Companions*

Kim Gek Lin Short, *The Bugging Watch & Other Exhibits*

Kim Gek Lin Short, *China Cowboy*

Shelly Taylor, *Black-Eyed Heifer*

Max Winter, *The Pictures*

Andrew Zornoza, *Where I Stay*

CHAPBOOKS

Sandy Florian, *32 Pedals and 47 Stops*
James Haug, *Scratch*
Claire Hero, *Dollyland*
Paula Koneazny, *Installation*
Paul McCormick, *The Exotic Moods of Les Baxter*
Teresa K. Miller, *Forever No Lo*
Jeanne Morel, *That Crossing Is Not Automatic*
Andrew Michael Roberts, *Give Up*
Brandon Shimoda, *The Inland Sea*
Chad Sweeney, *A Mirror to Shatter the Hammer*
Emily Toder, *Brushes With*
G.C. Waldrep, *One Way No Exit*

&

Tarpaulin Sky Literary Journal
in print and online

www.tarpaulinsky.com